Other books by Obert Skye

THE CREATURE FROM MY CLOSET SERIES:

Wonkenstein

Potterwookiee

Pinocula

Katfish

The Lord of the Hat

Batneezer

THE WITHERWOOD REFORM SCHOOL SERIES:

Witherwood Reform School

Lost & Found

OBERT SKYE

GEEKED OUT

Christy Ottaviano Books

HENRY HOLT AND COMPANY

NEW YORK

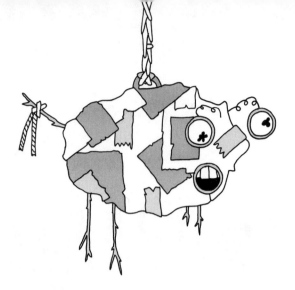

Henry Holt and Company, *Publishers since 1866*
Henry Holt® is a registered trademark of Macmillan Publishing Group, LLC
175 Fifth Avenue, New York, NY 10010
mackids.com

Library of Congress Cataloging-in-Publication Data is available.

ISBN 978-1-62779-939-3

Our books may be purchased in bulk for promotional, educational, or
business use. Please contact your local bookseller or the Macmillan Corporate
and Premium Sales Department at (800) 221-7945 ext. 5442 or by e-mail at
MacmillanSpecialMarkets@macmillan.com.

First edition, 2018 / Designed by Carol Ly
Printed in the United States of America by LSC Communications,
Harrisonburg, Virginia.
1   3   5   7   9   10   8   6   4   2

To Matt, the coolest, geekiest
person I've ever known.
You are missed every moment.

Contents

Gather your spears and textbooks.
We're going in.

CHAPTER ONE

The Ruin

The world is coming to an end. Or maybe it's just a phase—it's hard to tell. Things could smooth out in a couple of hundred years, but at the moment things are a mess, and the worst of it is that we still have to go to school. Seriously, if you think your school is hard, try going to one when society has fallen apart.

How did the world fall apart? Well, I'm glad I asked that. To begin with, things weren't going well all over the planet. Governments were fighting about things that they thought mattered, and people were polluting places that they thought didn't matter. People were unhappy and society and technology seemed to be getting out of hand. Then, as if things weren't tough enough, something happened that unraveled everything. You see, there are some very, very, very popular books called the Sand Thrower series.

The books are about a boy and a girl who travel through time by throwing sand and occasionally kissing. I'm not a huge fan, but almost all the girls (and a ton of boys) are obsessed with them.

A few years ago the Sand Thrower movie franchise released their third movie, *Grainy*. The first two movies were really good and kids loved them. But, the third movie blew chunks. I mean, it really stunk—like a dead skunk that's been sprayed with my grandmother's perfume and rolled in bad eggs. It was the best book in the series, but they made it into the worst movie ever! Because it stunk so bad society went bonkers. Fans all over the world left the theaters and took to the streets. They tore things up. Not even the cops could stop people from weeping and interrupting society with their sad selfies and uncontrollable behavior.

It was the beginning of the end.

The nonstop texting and online complaining caused hundreds of communications satellites to drop out of orbit and come crashing to earth. The failed satellites did massive amounts of damage and helped throw society into the toilet for many months. Governments couldn't communicate, people started more wars, and all systems experienced breakdowns. Factories and fires pumped out waste and smoke that made the weather bonkers. Everything fell apart, and the whole world changed—countries crumbled, states went to pieces, and neighborhoods got picked apart.

It was the end of one world and the start of another.

Now the government is bigger, and our streets are ruled by packs of unhappy, unsatisfied, and pushy fangirls and fanboys that society calls Fanatics. Most Fanatics spend their days silently stewing and aggressively taking selfies. Some attack people in outfits they don't like or chase down anyone who dares to say the third Sand Thrower movie is better than the book.

It's crazy. Middle school is hard enough, but add the breakdown of society to the daily grind, and it gets even stickier. I shouldn't complain too much. At least I'm lucky to be part of a group at school. The group I'm talking about is the AV Club. It used to stand for Audio Visual Club, but now it stands for Avoid Violence Club, because that's what we spend most of our day doing. We're thinkers, not fighters, and there are four of us: me, Mindy, Owen, and Xennitopher.

Tip   Mindy   Owen   Xen

Owen is older than all of us by almost half a year. He has about a dozen people in his family and doesn't like to go home because his big brothers pick on him. He doesn't like to do things that are hard because it makes his skin turn red and his nose run. He's kind and also kind of slow moving. According to the school aptitude test we had to take a few weeks ago, he would be best suited in a job where he didn't have to interact with others.

Xennitopher is my brother from another mother. He is

probably the coolest member of the AV Club. His hair always looks perfect, and he knows how to code in four languages. I've also seen him lift things that look heavy. His dad works for the mayor of Piggsburg and his mother works at the zoo protecting the animals from poachers.

Don't tell anyone, but Mindy is my favorite. We sort of have a thing. I mean, she sort of likes me as a friend. She was born in Japan and moved to Piggsburg shortly before the world unraveled. She is the glue in the AV Club. And not the cheap kind of glue they use at our school, but the kind of glue that could adhere a steam train to a steel rail. She's incredibly smart, and I wouldn't be surprised if someday we got married.

My name is Timothy Dover, but everyone calls me Tip, as in Tip Dover. It works because sometimes I have a hard time standing up without tripping. I used to mind the nickname, but now I'm fine with it and even kind of like it. I am an only child, and I have never fit in other than in the AV Club. Which is strange, because I'm a Fourth Master Elf in the *Elf Scrimmage* role-playing game, and you would think that would get me some respect, but it doesn't.

Our school is called Otto Waddle Jr. High Government Outpost, but we all call it WADD. The nickname works because our mascot is a weird wad-shaped creature, plus the school itself is a large wad of confusion.

Because my friends and I have high IQs, most of the school calls us Geeks and they give us a ton of grief. I guess being smart at WADD is uncool. I don't know which one of us Geeks is the smartest, but I was the only one who could figure out how to open the lid on Owen's asthma medicine.

BREATHE
RIGHT
PILLS

Twist twice to the left and once to the right. Squeeze bottle against the wall. Burp your name out loud and then shake like a rattle. Sing a song about kittens. Do not take if sleeping.

Also, I got an A, plus a handful of rice, in yesterday's Identifying Edible Weeds class. It was an important test. You might not be aware of this, but knowing the difference between edible and inedible things can save your life.

DANDELION   BAMBOO   SHRIMP AND PEA FLAVORED RAMEN

Eat   Eat   DO NOT EAT

WADD used to be a normal, boring school where people learned things about math and science instead of weeds and life-or-death kickball. When I think of how things used to be, I get a little nostalgic—which is a better-than-average way of saying I long for the old days. Sure, it's cool now to be able to bring spears to school, but I wouldn't mind not having to make my own erasers from old grease squeezed out of last week's maybe-meat loaf.

Could you squeeze some more? I've made a lot of mistakes.

Even getting to school these days can be an adventure. I have to walk through hordes of Fanatics taking aggressive selfies and dodge stray animals and government workers. Then, when I get here, I'm forced to go through security, which is just a big hole in the wall. It's the one way into our school, and you can only bring in what you can fit through the opening. At WADD it's perfectly acceptable for people to bring sticks or eggs or torches to school, but the security hole helps keep out the big things like four-wheelers and tanks.

I don't usually worry about getting through security, but this morning I was packing something more than just my inhaler and tablet. Today I had a bag filled with melted-down eraser grease. The reason for bringing the goop was because me and the AV Club were going to teach Nerf, the leader of the Jocks, a messy lesson. He'd been trouble for a while, and because our school let him get away with everything, it was up to us to teach him some manners.

These days everything is more extreme and crazy than it used to be. Our school is filled with extreme clubs, groups, cliques, and confusion. There's the Jocks, and the Goths, and the Sox—which is a group of students who no longer wear shoes. There are the Loners and the Freaks and the Pens—a group of wannabe writers who meet behind the wall of broken desks near the cafeteria. There are a few more groups, including the Staffers, which is made up of all the teachers and the staff. I guess they're necessary because they teach us stuff that the government thinks we need to know to survive in this brave new world.

Our school is a government outpost where only the strong survive. The Staffers try to teach, but they also have to fight and reason with us. For example, last month there was a big chair debacle at WADD. The Staffers took all the seats and built forts out of them so they could hide and be protected from unruly students while teaching.

Since none of us enjoyed standing or sitting on hard floors, some of the cliques joined together and duct taped the Staffers' cars. But the protest didn't work. The Staffers used butter knives and cut their doors open and peeled the tape off of their windows. And because most of their cars were junkers to begin with, they were happy to have vehicles that looked tough and durable.

I wasn't concerned with the Staffers today. They'd been pretty calm lately, and most of them didn't mind me, due to the fact that I never acted up. No, my concern was with Nerf. We Geeks were going to take him down and move from the lowest group at our school to the highest. Over the last few months, we'd been working on a brilliant plan to put the Jocks in their place. And when we pranked them, we would become the top dogs and finally get the respect we deserved.

The Jocks are the most obnoxious group at WADD. They think the school is their playground and that they're the only ones who matter. They're always playing sports in the halls and tackling people who are just trying to make their way to classrooms. They push around the Sox, mess with the Pens, and mock the Goths. And they dislike us Geeks the most, which is why it's our responsibility to do something about it. Nobody's ever given them grief before—until today.

If you think I'm being harsh, it might help to know that Nerf, the leader of the Jocks, is easily the worst person at WADD. When he walks down the hall, most of the students hide behind the big safety mounds made out of old textbooks. Nerf is best known for dishing out painful high fives.

Even if you don't give a rat's backside about sports, he still makes you high-five him. And if you fail to high-five him? Well, I'll just say two words—*low five*. And trust me, the low five is way worse than the high—WAY WORSE!

The Jocks are bad enough, but Nerf and his two best friends, Mud and Weasel, take the cake and then cram it in your face.

They're always locking us in lockers, or stealing our torches, or smashing our tablets over their heads. They eat first at lunch, get the best pencils, and roam the halls belching their stupid fight song.

Sadly, I'm one of their favorite people to pick on. I'm too skinny, too pale, too weird, and 200 percent smarter than them. Every chance they get, they tip me over. Nerf and his pals are equally mean to the rest of the AV Club. We might be the smallest student group at WADD, but we get picked on the most.

It's a scientific fact that people can only take being bullied for so long. We've tried reasoning with the Jocks, but the debates always end up with us having our heads put into the toilets or our tablets thrown into the pond next to the school.

Reasoning had failed, so it was payback time. That's why we Geeks were marching though Q Hall, the main and longest hall at WADD, and heading toward the cafeteria. We weren't going there to eat; we just needed to pick something up. We really never ate in the cafeteria because it was horrible. (Sorry, Lunch Lady Sniddle.) The food was disgusting, the floors were sticky, and almost every week a food fight broke out between two warring groups. Last Wednesday the Goths ambushed the Pens and won back their moping spot near the school library. It was a long food fight, but the Goths were victorious.

Sometimes the Goths worry me, but they're nothing compared to the Jocks, and even though the Jocks are mostly horrible, there is one person at WADD who I'd ship out first.

Most schools are led by their principal. Not at WADD. Our principal is a frightened pushover who spends his days hiding under tables and behind walls just hoping that the students will go away.

Principal Woth doesn't scare anyone. The person who scares everyone is the school secretary, Mrs. Susan.

Mrs. Susan has more control over WADD than anyone else. She also doesn't like any of the students except for the Jocks. Us Geeks are probably her least favorite. I think she feels we're smarter than her and that makes her angry.

Her desk is in the office at the front of the school and at the beginning of Q Hall. I actually should say her desks, because she put her own on top of desks she stole from other teachers. She sits up there on her throne looking down at us, always ready to punish someone for something.

Mrs. Susan likes to sit at her desks and make random announcements on the intercom. But the intercom speakers are so bad that she always sounds like Darth Vader. Which is why most of us call her Darth Susan behind her back.

As we were walking to the cafeteria, the intercom crackled to life.

Don't forget we will be taking the SLAP in two days. Also the Supply War begins today at one fifteen. Attendance is mandatory.

Mrs. Susan's voice caused us to stop walking for a second. I didn't really like thinking about Darth Susan or the Supply War, because what we were about to do could easily become the biggest mistake of our lives, and hearing her voice reminded me of how scared I really was.

I shook it off and we continued on our quest.

CHAPTER TWO

Greased Up

WADD doesn't have a bell system. There's the intercom for Darth Susan and her personal announcements, but no bells. What we do have is Finn the school crier.

Bells can be considered alarms, and these days any sounding alarm usually means something bad is happening. If the government is imposing a surprise curfew, we'll hear an alarm scream down from some drones up above. If there's a loose cannon in the neighborhood, the drones will be set off as well.

If the air gets too polluted with hair spray and mousse from hordes of Fanatics, there's a government siren for that. So, Finn, the school crier, sits up in his tower and shouts out whenever class periods are over or any other message that needs to be heard by all of WADD.

Usually I didn't mind hearing him scream, but the announcement that lunch was over and the Supply War would begin made my heart flip.

Owen was even more scared about what was coming up. Of course, Owen was scared of everything. I once saw him almost pass out when a sock puppet looked at him weird.

Owen didn't think we'd be successful in our quest to make the Jocks look bad, because they were popular and those kind of people never look bad.

You should know that *log* is a word that most of my schoolmates use to describe people we don't like. And Nerf is a log times two (a double log, if you will) and he has been ruling the school for too long. You should also know that Owen says *splimp* too much. It's a word he made up once after simultaneously stubbing his toe and sneezing. We've tried to make him stop, but he thinks it's clever.

We stopped off at the cafeteria to quickly swipe something and then headed to the back of the school. The four of us gathered in the burned-out storage shed that had been destroyed months ago by a group of Fanatics.

I set the large bag of grease down, and we all began to transfer it into the secret places we had stitched into our clothes. We weren't allowed to bring backpacks or bags to the Supply War, so hiding the grease was a necessity.

For the record, we're usually one of the cleaner groups at school. It's not always easy to take a shower these days, thanks to water rations. Plus, most people use their bathtubs to store grain. At least we try not to be disgusting. The Sox, on the other hand, don't wash their socks, which makes it hard to be around them.

I had altered my pants last night. I let my mom help me sew hidden pockets into the lining. She thought she was assisting me with a science project, but as everyone knows, sewing is not a true science, and if it were, I wouldn't need my mom's help. I was a whiz at sewing and at science, while my mom struggles with trash-quilting or solving the DNA mysteries in the *Weekly End Times* newspaper.

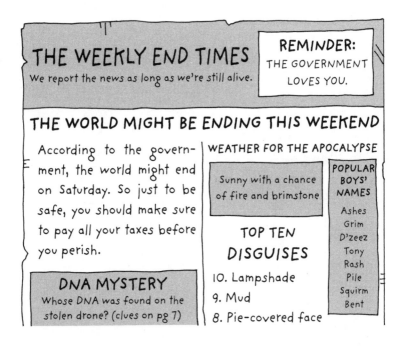

THE WEEKLY END TIMES

We report the news as long as we're still alive.

REMINDER: THE GOVERNMENT LOVES YOU.

THE WORLD MIGHT BE ENDING THIS WEEKEND

According to the government, the world might end on Saturday. So just to be safe, you should make sure to pay all your taxes before you perish.

DNA MYSTERY

Whose DNA was found on the stolen drone? (clues on pg 7)

WEATHER FOR THE APOCALYPSE

Sunny with a chance of fire and brimstone

TOP TEN DISGUISES

10. Lampshade
9. Mud
8. Pie-covered face

POPULAR BOYS' NAMES

Ashes
Grim
D'zeez
Tony
Rash
Pile
Squirm
Bent

Sewing might not be a true science, but it's an essential life skill. With society falling apart, people are now forced to sew their own tents, clothes, and intruder-trapping nets.

That's one of the reasons why everyone dresses so strangely these days. People will wear anything they can find that might protect them or make them feel safer. Some people wear pans for hats and strap things like books and pieces of metal to them for extra protection against attackers. I don't go for any of that fancy stuff. But I do know how to sew, because it's pretty much impossible to find anything well made at any of the department stores.

It's equally hard to find medical help. Sometimes we even have to stitch up cuts because the local hospital is overcrowded with people who have concussions from selfie sticks or teenagers who think they're turning into zombies.

As soon as we were all filled up with grease, I took a moment to look us over. My pants were full, Xen had two small pouches under his armpits, Mindy had some in her lunch box, and Owen's shirt was filled to the brim.

I didn't know what success smelled like, but at the moment, I was hoping it smelled like grease.

CHAPTER THREE
The Plan

Once a month, the government delivers school supplies to WADD by drone. They fly up above our town in waves and drop off things like paper and pens and emergency flares to schools and other workplaces.

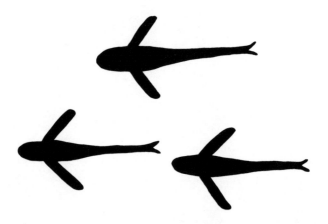

Because Darth Susan is the school secretary, she's in charge of dividing up the supplies and splitting them evenly among the teachers. It's supposed to be a simple thing. Unfortunately, Darth Susan enjoys seeing people in battle, so she holds what she calls a Supply War. It's like a football game, but with fewer rules, and school supplies instead of a ball. The teachers take on the Jocks, and the team who scores the most gets to keep all of the supplies for that month. The winning team also gets to stand on a podium at the end of the war game and bust open a piñata that's shaped like our school mascot and made out of old homework and garbage.

THE WADD

The whole event is really dumb. Plus, Darth Susan cheats. She always makes sure that the Jocks win, and when they do, they turn all of the supplies over to her. That way she can continue to control every tablet and piece of paper in the school.

The Staffers have no chance of winning. Not with the dirty tricks Darth Susan pulls. Last month she made sure that the Staffers' uniforms shrank before the game so it was hard for them to lift their arms. A month earlier, the Staffers were given spoiled doughnuts before the game, and they all threw up.

And the month before that, the Staffers were informed that if they wanted to get paid, they had to lose. No teacher at WADD can afford to have their salary cut by even a single chicken.

So the Staffers pretend to try, but they always lose.

The whole school is forced to attend the Supply War whether we want to or not. It's held on the weed-covered football field, and we all sit on the rusty bleachers. Darth Susan thinks that if we view the game we'll see just how hard it is to get supplies. That way we'll be more grateful for the few things we might eventually end up with.

This time, however, the Supply War was going to end a bit differently than usual. True, we Geeks didn't like to mess with people, but eventually you have to put a stop to stupidity, and Nerf was stupid times ten thousand.

"Does that mean we're going to have to depants his head and show the world what he really is?" Owen asked.

"Don't worry about that," Mindy said. "Let's just be

excited. Nerf asked for this, and on a scale of one to ten, I'm eight-point-seven pumped."

Owen gulped, Xen whimpered, and I took a couple of extra pumps of my inhaler. Mindy was the bravest member of our group. She was different from most girls at our school. Not only was she super smart, she loved things like bugs and books, and hated the Sand Thrower series.

We're pretty glad that Mindy's a member of the AV Club. I probably shouldn't say this, but I think she flirts with me sometimes. For example, last week, right after she and I had taught a couple of Staffers how to use their tablets, she turned to me and said,

That's flirting, right?

I guess we kind of have a thing. Just don't tell Owen or Xen, because I think they think that she has a thing for them. Some people are so naïve, which is an above-average way of saying Owen and Xen are fooling themselves and I'm not.

I checked the time on my phone.

"We'd better get going," I said.

It wouldn't be long now before the Supply War began, and we needed to have our stuff in place.

"Ready?" I asked.

All three of my friends nodded. We were greased up and raring to go.

CHAPTER FOUR

The Dark Arts

The AV Club played a small role in setting up for the Supply War. We did only one thing, and that was make sure there was a working microphone on the stage at the north end of the football field. The microphone was for Darth Susan to talk into, and setting it up was an easy job that also gave us access to the field before everyone arrived.

"Nerf's going to remember this day forever," I whispered with excitement.

"The smell of the grease is making me hungry," Owen whispered back.

When we got to the field, Tyler, the janitor, was standing by the gate. Tyler had been assigned by the government to clean our outpost. The problem is that he's not very good at cleaning. Even some of the simplest tasks confuse him. He's not the hardest worker, either, and he scares the grease out of me.

Tyler was also supposed to guard the gate and make sure that nobody brought any backpacks or other bags onto the field. But just like cleaning, he stunk at the job. We bribed him with the muffin Mindy had smuggled from the lunchroom and then invited him to go eat it somewhere else.

"You're welcome to go eat it in private," I suggested. "We'll watch the field."

Fine. You kids set up.
I'm going to go take a nap
behind the dumpsters.

Tyler always wears a trash can over his head. Everyone thinks he's hiding something, but I heard it's because he's embarrassed about being bald. He stuck the muffin up into his trash can and took a big sniff.

"Yum, plain flavored."

Tyler walked off to eat his new bribe. The muffin really wasn't necessary, because he usually had no problem leaving us alone on the field. He trusted us because we were Geeks, and according to all the movies Tyler had ever seen, geeks rarely did anything mischievous.

Today that was going to change.

The four of us walked across the field, leaking grease and making our way to the platform on the north end. Once we got there, it took only a couple of seconds to hook up the microphone and get the generator running. Then we hid under the platform and waited for the Dark Arts Club to arrive.

The Dark Arts Club always makes the celebratory WADD piñata. Their name is deceiving because they don't actually dabble in the dark arts. They're just a group of students who are into regular arts. But since our school never gets things like paints or markers, and because Darth Susan doesn't like creativity, kids in Dark Arts have to paint with charcoal, old coffee grounds, and used toner. Which means that all of their paintings are a bit dark.

The Dark Arts Club makes the piñata because papier-mâché is a kind of art. The piñata is ugly, waddish, and sad-looking. It's also filled with old homework that's been shredded into confetti-size pieces, and it's hung up over the platform so that it's ready to shower the winners of the Supply War with glory.

As expected, two Dark Arters arrived on time to hang up their creation. From below the platform we could hear them talking.

I took out my phone and quickly sent a text to Peter, the leader of the Dark Arts. I heard his phone beep when he received my text. He seemed overly surprised that someone was trying to contact him.

"Who's texting you?" Peter's friend asked. "I've never heard you get a message."

"I don't know," he said. "Only my mom texts me and she's busy foraging for batteries near the old hardware store."

Peter read the text aloud and cheered. I guess he liked what he saw.

"We gotta go," Peter said excitedly.

They hung up the piñata in record time while chatter-ing about how pumped they were at the possibility of real art supplies. As soon as the piñata was in place, they ran off, leaving us alone under the platform.

"So far, so good," I whispered to my friends.

We quickly climbed out from under the stage, and Xen stood guard while Owen and I lowered the piñata back down. I untied it and held it in my arms.

Hurry, let's get this thing filled up.

47

Owen took out a pair of safety scissors his little sister had scored last week at her elementary school supply assembly. He started to cut a hole in the top of the piñata.

"I'm nervous," Xen whispered while still on the lookout. "I think I'm about to hyperventilate. And my body temperature is off by three degrees."

"Yeah," Owen added as he finished cutting the opening. "My ankles are sweating like mad. Maybe we should just run away and pretend like we were never going to do this."

"We can't stop," I said, trying to sound brave. "Owen, do you remember when Nerf pantsed you in front of the girls' competitive trench-digging team?"

"The girls still call me Grandpa Panties," Owen sniffled.

"And you, Mindy—didn't Nerf keep making fun of you during your last bad hair day?"

"It wasn't my fault. I ran out of styling gel, so I had to use tree sap."

"And, Xen, remember when Nerf stole your glasses and underwear from your gym locker and welded your glasses onto the statue in the park?"

Xen nodded with humiliation.

"We have to do this," I said, using my bravest voice.

49

We took the grease out and poured it into the opening. The smelly stuff oozed in, covering the confetti and filling the entire wad. Xen plugged up the top of the piñata, and as a team we retied it and hoisted it back up above the platform. It was not easy to lift. By my calculations, it weighed 27.3 pounds. And we aren't exactly the strongest kids in school—we're like the opposite of buff, which is biff. Still, we huffed and puffed and pulled until it was back up and hanging in its spot.

I could tell we were scared because my heart was beating like mad and Owen's breathing sounded like a science experiment on the verge of an explosion. Even though I was nervous, I was also excited. I had never pulled a practical joke on anyone. Plenty of jokes had been played on me, but now it was my time to be practically joking.

CHAPTER FIVE

The Supply War

At one o'clock, the students began storming through the open gate and took their places on the bleachers. We sat down at the spot reserved for Geeks. Once both sides of the benches were filled, Darth Susan stepped up onto the platform and took hold of the microphone.

Usually this was the most nerve-racking part of the Supply War for us. After all, it was the AV Club's job to make sure the microphone worked. If it didn't, we would be held personally responsible and forced to work the weed fields behind the school.

"Attention, dear students," Darth Susan said. "Everyone please calm down."

Nobody did.

Shut your *sweet traps*, or *I'll* see that the school vending machines are destroyed and replaced with a flaming pile of tires.

Everyone stopped making noise and looked on with fear. I didn't like hearing her screech at us, but I was relieved that the microphone worked. And since the microphone worked, the Supply War could begin. And since the Supply War could begin, Nerf could win. And when Nerf won, it would be a storm of grease and confetti raining on him.

"This is crazy, Tip," Xen said. "I can't believe we're actually doing this."

"It's like something Nerf would do," Mindy added. "He does stuff like this all the time."

"Exactly," I said. "We're giving him a taste of his own medicine."

"My medicine tastes like peppermint chalk," Xen added needlessly.

Xen is the newest member of the AV Club. He came to

our school last year after his father got a job working for the government here in Piggsburg. He is incredibly smart, but also insecure about not being as tall as the rest of us. He ties books to his feet to make himself a bit taller and wears old cookie sheets on his chest for protection. It is nice having him around. One of his biggest contributions to our AV Club was when he designed the logo for us. Now he always has it painted on his outfits.

It's a simple but elegant logo.

Darth Susan kept talking into the microphone. She said a bunch of things about how great our school was and how lucky we were to have a place to get educated. She talked about the state of our society and how it was an honor and a privilege to get school supplies these days. She then said a few words about the Staffers who would be trying to win some supplies for themselves. I looked over at the teachers. They were lined up on one side of the field, looking unhappy and defeated before the game had even begun.

Darth Susan gave a little speech about Nerf and the Jocks and how brave they were to be fighting for us, the students. As she spoke, the Jocks took the field while the school band blew the few instruments they had. Everyone in the bleachers stomped and cheered.

I wanted to boo, but even in these times of chaos and distress, I still have a hard time not using good manners. So maybe I didn't boo, but I did stand my ground by not clapping. I was like that ancient Scottish guy who once fought for freedom by doing something. Of course, I don't know what it was he did exactly because our teachers had never won any history books in any of the Supply Wars to teach us properly.

The referee for the Supply War was Mr. Upwonder. All he did during the game was blow a whistle and beg the Jocks to stop running so fast or scoring so often.

Mr. Upwonder walked out to the middle of the field, looked up into the sky, and blew his whistle twice.

A large drone flew in over the field and released a bundle of supplies that dropped to the ground with a small parachute.

Everyone cheered as the goods hit the field.

From what I could see, it looked like a decent assortment of supplies this month. There were reams of paper and bundles of rubber bands. There were also some books and charge cords and even a few tablets.

"Looks like a good load," Mindy yelled.

"I'll say," I yelled back. "I think I see a six-pack of Sharpies."

Mr. Upwonder picked up a ream of paper from the pile

and carried it out to the middle of the field. He placed it on the tee and stepped back. From the stage Darth Susan yelled,

Upwonder blew his whistle again, and all the Jocks ran down the field. Nerf kicked off the first pack of paper to the Staffers.

Not to stick up for Nerf, but it's actually really hard to kick a pack of paper. It went about two feet, and Nerf picked it up and ran the rest of the way down the field for a touchdown.

Staffers zero, Jocks one. I repeat, the Staffers are zeros.

The game didn't get any more exciting than that. The Jocks kicked off a box of tape and then the teachers caught it. Mr. Rack, the Lifestyle-Deathstyle teacher, fumbled the tape, and Weasel took it in for a touchdown. They kept kicking things and then knocking Staffers over. In less than twenty minutes, Nerf and his team had scored all of the supplies and the teachers were defeated.

Darth Susan stepped up to the microphone and instructed Nerf to come up onto the stage and break the ceremonial WADD piñata.

This was it!

Nerf strutted his way to the platform.

Everyone in the bleachers cheered as if he had actually done something more impressive than just kicking tape and pens around to win a bunch of supplies for Mrs. Susan. Now she would make the Staffers do all sorts of embarrassing things if they ever wanted new pencils or textbooks.

Nerf climbed up onto the platform, and Darth Susan handed him the sacred wadd-beating stick.

I looked over at Owen—he was sweating and shaking. He reminded me of Dindo the elf king from the *Elf Scrimmage* role-playing game. He was the main elf, but he was always sweating and shaking because everything scared him.

Vomit rising! Must run and hide from everything!

I felt queasy, but I had to keep reminding myself that we were about to right a ton of wrongs with a piñata full of grease.

Nerf stepped up onto a small box below the piñata. He smiled at the crowd and then flexed his muscles. Typical Nerf. Some girls swooned while some boys felt bad about themselves. He lifted the stick o' celebration over his head and prepared to swing. Mindy closed her eyes, and Owen bit his nails. I couldn't look away—I wanted to see that grease cover him like the dumb double log he was.

Nerf started to swing and then . . .

CHAPTER SIX

Sabotage!

He stopped? He stopped swinging? What was going on?

The crowd gasped in surprise.

"What's happening?" Xen asked.

"I have no idea why he didn't hit it," I answered.

It made no sense for Nerf to pause—he loved cracking open the piñata. It was his thing. He always cracked it open and then did a stupid chicken dance.

"Maybe he's just repositioning his hands on the stick," Owen suggested. "You know, in preparation for taking an extra-big swing."

Nerf stepped down off the box, smiling like he had swallowed something incredibly delicious. Darth Susan nodded and handed him the microphone.

"Fellow students," he said loudly.

The crowd began to murmur.

"I know we won the Supply War," Nerf continued. "And this is the part where I usually beat the snot out of the piñata. But today is gonna be different."

"What's going on?" Xen said as he began to sweat like Owen and Dindo.

Today Mrs. Susan wants me to share the honor of breaking the wadd. Some people in our school never get to break things because they're kinda lame and not good at sports like the Jocks.

My stomach did the kind of flips my body would never be capable of doing in real life.

I was pretty lame.

I wasn't very good at sports.

The hair on the back of my neck stood up, and my head felt dizzy.

"So," Nerf continued, "Mrs. Susan would like the . . . Geeks of the AV Club to have the honor of splitting the wadd today."

Everyone turned to look at us. Most of the groups in school had certain sections in the bleachers where they sat during the Supply War—the Goths sat where it was shadiest, the Loners sat up high in the far corner, and the Sox sat on the bottom row so that they could slide their hands and feet against the rails. Us Geeks sat near the bottom of the bleachers next to the port-a-potties. That way we could be close to the platform if we needed to assist with the microphone. Also it put us near the bathroom, which helps Xen take care of his relaxed bladder if he needs to.

It's my only weakness—
well, that and my fear of whistling.

The crowd began to boo.

Apparently they were not happy about the thought of us Geeks breaking the piñata. Most students had the same kind of lukewarm feelings for us that Nerf did.

The crowd moaned and hollered while I tried to process what was happening. We break the piñata? We break the piñata full of grease? We break the piñata in front of our whole school?

"Come on up here, Tip," Nerf ordered. "And bring your friends."

All four of us stayed seated in the bleachers and shook our heads.

"Mrs. Susan must have found out about the grease," Mindy whispered in a panic.

"How could she?" Owen asked me.

"I have no idea."

"Get up here," Nerf commanded through the microphone. "Let's see how hard you can hit this wadd."

"Maybe Mrs. Susan's just trying to embarrass us," I suggested. "She probably thinks we can't even break that thing open."

"We probably can't," Owen said. "The Dark Arts Club uses a lot of paste. I could barely cut through it."

"Come up here now!" Nerf insisted.

All four of us nervously stood as the crowd simultaneously booed and cheered. They were all thirsty for confetti.

We walked down the bleachers and over to the platform.

As we stepped up, I saw Darth Susan with Nerf standing right next to her. She was smiling so sweetly that it made my teeth ache. She winked as if to say, *You're going to do great*. Then she winked again to say, *You're going down*. She was an excellent dual-purpose winker. I gulped and pushed at my nose like I was wearing glasses. Nerf reached out and handed the stick to me.

"Why don't you do the honors, Tip?" Darth Susan said. "You can stand on the box while the rest of your little group stands around you."

"I don't think that would be fair," I said, hoping to talk my way out of this. "We didn't win the supplies—Nerf did. He's the hero. Let him hit it."

"Well, aren't you sweet?" she cooed. "Now, climb up

onto that box and don't get down until that wadd's good and broken."

We were doomed. And not doomed like the planet currently was with all the craziness in the streets and society falling apart. We were doomed like four kids who were out of their element. Geeks who had foolishly tried to pull off a practical joke that was about to backfire miserably.

We shuffled across the platform to the box.

I stepped up onto the box while Mindy, Owen, and Xen circled around me. I'll be honest, which is something I always try to be: This felt like a terrible moment—maybe our worst day ever. Sure, there was the time we had hooked up the school's computers to the wrong generator and accidentally blew up three monitors, but this felt worse.

Nerf began chanting with the crowd, "Hit the wadd, hit the wadd, hit the wadd!"

The entire student body joined, and soon my ears were ringing with the chant. I looked up at the piñata that was now hanging directly above me.

Some of the grease was starting to seep through the bottom, and a big fat drop smacked me in the right eye. I wiped it away and glanced around, wondering where Principal Woth was.

"Hit the wadd, hit the wadd, hit the wadd!" the crowd continued to shout.

"Just get it over with," Mindy cried.

The screams got even louder. "Hit the wadd, hit the wadd!"

"This is probably my fault," Owen sobbed.

Owen always blames everything bad on himself. I think he feels that it's somehow his fault that the third Sand Thrower movie is so awful. Owen is just that kind of person. He's smart, but sometimes he thinks life would be easier if he were less smart and didn't have to think about things. Now he was overthinking what was happening.

"This is not your fault, Owen," I said as a second grease drop smacked me on top of the head. "This mess belongs to me. I should never have suggested it."

I looked up and summoned the courage of Beltcrazan, who is a human/robot hybrid in the *Elf Scrimmage* game. Whenever Beltcrazan gets in a pinch, he plugs his right leg into a wall socket and says,

I summon the courage of myself!

Saying the words out loud made me feel a little braver, and when a third grease drop plunked down on my eyes,

I pulled the stick back and forcefully swung. It wasn't the hardest hit, but the piñata was so saturated that even my lame whack caused the wadd to burst and shower us with old smelly grease.

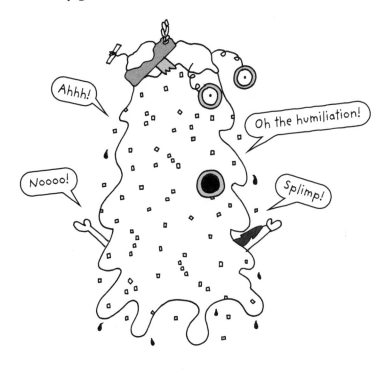

The crowd loved the oily surprise. They cheered and screamed as gray, goo-covered confetti filled every crevasse and crook of our bodies.

Darth Susan declared the Supply War officially over and instructed Nerf and his team to take all the supplies they had won to her office. The rest of the school exited the bleachers and made their way back to their classes. We four Geeks remained on the platform looking like greasy nerds.

I guess I wasn't surprised that the entire school had laughed at us—that happened pretty often. I also wasn't surprised to be covered in foul oil—because now my outsides felt as awful as my ins.

I wiped grease from my eyes and looked over at Nerf. Before he left the platform, he turned to take one last look in our direction.

CHAPTER SEVEN

Hunted Down

Everyone cleared out from the football field and returned to the school. It had been loud and overwhelming, and now it was just silent and depressing. Tyler, the janitor, approached us. He seemed unfazed to see the four of us standing there covered with greasy confetti.

I told Mrs. Susan you were leaking stuff and messing with the piñata.

Also, I'm not cleaning any of you up.

Tyler had ratted us out! He was a lousy janitor but a pretty good snitch.

I wanted to be angry, but I was too sticky to throw a fit. The grease made it incredibly difficult to walk away from

Tyler—one of us would slip, and then one of us would trip over that person, and another would pull the other down. We were like a less-coordinated bunch of greased pigs. Tyler was no help. He just stood there laughing as if we were the funniest mess he had ever seen. He even got out his phone and started filming.

I'm posting this right now. Hashtag epic Geek fail. Hashtag oily nerds.

I fell seven times before we reached the gym/bomb shelter where we knew the industrial showers were located. The showers were super powerful and were used for emergencies for when someone needed to hose off suspicious dust, or wash out their hair after being attacked in the streets by a gang of Fanatics doing makeovers.

We stood under the powerful water with all our clothes on and let it blast the grease and confetti off us.

It took only a couple of minutes, and when we were done, we no longer slipped while walking. We still smelled like grease, but our feet had traction.

"If my calculations are correct," Xen said, "I swallowed one-point-two pounds of that disgusting grease. My insides feel like a gas station restroom."

"If my calculations are correct, this day's been a bust," I added.

As we stepped out of the gym/bomb shelter with sopping-wet clothes and low spirits, the school intercom screeched to life, followed by the sound of Darth Susan's scary voice.

Attention, dear students, due to unfortunate selfishness by one of your peer groups, there will be extra homework for everyone.

"Uh-oh," I groaned.

"We will be cracking the whip and taking away privileges," Darth Susan continued. "All for your adorable personal safety. If you wish to thank someone for what's happening, you might take it up with the AV Club."

After she finished, the school crier shouted out from his post.

Fifth period is over.
Be thankful you're still alive!

A classroom door down the hall burst open, and Nerf, Weasel, and Mud stepped out of their Dystopian Baking class. Weasel spotted us and yelled, "Hey, Nerf, it's Tip and the Geeks. Let's go thank them hard."

We took off running down the hall.

I don't want to brag, but I'm actually a pretty good

runner. It's probably because I've had a lot of practice fleeing from bullies. Mindy's pretty good as well, but Owen's slow, and the books Xen ties to his feet to make himself taller don't exactly make him Dystopian Olympics material. But at the moment we were running like a team, a nonathletic, scared-out-of-our-wits team.

A couple more hallway doors opened, and other students joined Nerf in the chase. We dodged book bunkers and study hammocks as we scurried into the unlit cafeteria. Lunch was long over, and the room was shut down for the day. The floors were sticky and I could still smell the burnt asparagus and slightly expired tuna they had served for lunch. I considered running right through the cafeteria and out the far doors, but instead I jumped over the front counter and into the kitchen.

My friends did the same.

We crouched behind the counter hoping to hide. I desperately wanted to take out my inhaler to calm my breathing, but I was too nervous to move.

"If we're caught, it's wedgies for sure," Xen whispered.

"And toilet swirlies," Owen added.

"And low fives." I shuddered.

Nerf and his gang of not-well-wishers burst into the dark cafeteria, whooping and calling out our names.

Tip! Come out, come out, wherever you are. Owen, Mindy, Xennitopher, we all want to thank you for what you did today.

It would have been nice for a teacher to come into the cafeteria and save us, but that wasn't going to happen. Occasionally when things got out of hand, Staffers would stand near the trouble and hope the misbehaving students would knock it off. But at the moment, there were no Staffers to be found, and we were on our own.

"You Geeks have done it this time," Nerf continued. "You blew it."

I could hear people walking around the cafeteria, moving chairs and looking for us under tables. Someone threw something made of glass, and it shattered against a wall.

I motioned for my friends to follow me, and we began to quietly scurry farther back into the dark kitchen. I knew it was only a matter of moments before Nerf searched behind the counter, so we needed to hide for our lives. I wanted to go into the pantry, but when I opened the door, we were stopped by the sight of Principal Woth crouched behind a large box of irregular refried beans.

Don't tell them I'm here.

You might want to rethink being a principal.

We backed out of the pantry and over into the far corner of the kitchen. It was dark, but it was easy to tell that we had run out of room to move. We were trapped next to a refrigerator and a large metal cabinet labeled POTS and PANS.

"My shy bladder's relaxing," Xen warned us.

"Does anyone have a club or a spear?" I asked.

I saw someone jump over the counter and land in the kitchen. It was Nerf. We were done for. He opened the pantry door, and I heard Principal Woth pleading.

"Please leave me alone," he said.

"Sorry," Nerf replied.

Nerf closed the pantry door and began to walk in our direction.

I shifted and tried to squeeze between the refrigerator and the metal cabinet. As I squirmed, I felt the cabinet move. It pushed out slightly from the wall, and even in the dark, I saw that there was some sort of open space behind it.

Owen saw it too.

Without communicating, we pushed the cabinet out a few more inches, and all of us scrambled behind it and into the hidden area. Mindy and I pulled the cabinet back into place.

While I was trying to catch my breath, Mindy whispered, "What is this place?"

I didn't answer, so Nerf wouldn't hear us. Besides, I had no idea what the space was. It seemed to be a forgotten room hidden behind a cabinet.

"Keep looking for them," Nerf said from the other side of the cabinet. "Search everywhere."

We heard someone open the doors of the cabinet looking for us. But since we were behind it, they found nothing. Nerf said a few words that most parents don't like to hear and then closed the cabinet doors.

"There's nobody in the kitchen," he shouted.

"Maybe they evaporated," Weasel hollered back.

"Don't be dumb," Nerf said sarcastically. "They probably never came into the kitchen, or they went out the other door. But they didn't evaporate, whatever that means. Now let's check Q Hall."

Nerf barked some more orders, and I heard multiple footsteps scurrying away. After we were sure they were gone, all four of us took out our government-issued inhalers and pumped twice.

CHAPTER EIGHT
Bitten

"That was way too close," Mindy said while exhaling.

"And where are we?" I asked, taking out my phone and turning on the flashlight.

As the room came into view, we all gasped, and Mindy followed her gasp with a "wow."

The hidden room was actually not that impressive to look at. It was about the size of a normal bedroom but with low ceilings. There was nothing in it except for four large tin cans sitting in the middle of the floor.

"Splimp, do you think there's food in those?"

"Maybe," I replied.

"Do you think Lunch Lady Sniddle knows this room is here?" Mindy asked.

"I try not to think about Sniddle," I answered.

Owen stood up and walked over to the cans. He picked one of them up.

"It's empty."

The next two cans were empty as well, but the fourth one was heavy and full of something.

"It's got to be food. Forgotten food. That means nobody will miss it if it gets eaten."

"Really?" Xen asked in disbelief. "The whole school is looking to thank us hard, and you're thinking about food?"

"Why not?" Owen asked. "I'm always thinking about food. Besides, we've got time. I'm not leaving this room. No way. I plan on sneaking out when everyone's gone and heading home without getting beat up. Hopefully by tomorrow people will have found something else to worry about other than us. In fact, maybe the world will finally end, and we won't have to bother with any of this."

"That's actually a really sound plan," Xen admitted. "It reduces our chances of humiliation by over twenty-three percent."

"Of course it's sound," Owen bragged. "I came up with it. Years of being a coward have made me clever." We sat in silence for a while before boredom made all of us antsy.

Owen took out his pocket rock.

Gently, he began to tap the top edge of the fourth tin can. When it didn't immediately pop open, he started to tap harder. When that didn't work, he went at the can like it contained a working lightsaber or a cheat code to the game *Muffin Warrior*, which we had been playing for months and still couldn't beat.

"You need to bang quieter," I begged. "Someone might hear us."

"Splimp, it's sealed tight."

Owen pounded the can as hard as he could. It took some real whacking, but after a dozen more hits, the top finally cracked open around the edge. Owen hammered the lid back.

We all stood and walked over.

I shone my phone on the now-open can.

Inside was a green chunky substance.

"That's disgusting," Mindy said. "Ugggh."

"It doesn't smell that bad," Owen said.

"It doesn't smell like anything," I pointed out.

"That's what I mean," Owen insisted. "It smells like nothing, and nothing doesn't stink."

"Actually," Xen interjected, "it's been proven that even nothing has an odor, and you can . . ."

Xen stopped talking, because Owen had put his pointer finger into the green goo and was pulling it back out. Whatever the substance was, it didn't look like *nothing*.

I noticed that there was a date stamped on the side of the can.

"Look at that date," I said. "That stuff's over thirty years old."

Owen held his finger up to his nose and took a sniff. He then shrugged and opened his mouth.

"Don't do it!" Mindy insisted. "DON'T—"

It was too late. Owen stuck his finger into his mouth and licked off the green ooze. Sure, there wasn't a lot of extra food these days, but I didn't think things were bad enough to go eating thirty-year-old green goo. We all watched Owen with expressions of horror. Surprisingly, he didn't die, or even make a sour face.

"It's not bad."

Owen reached his hand into the large can and pulled out a big fat chunk of goo. Before any of us could say anything, he bit right into it. It was one of the most disturbing things I've ever seen—and these days, I see a lot of disturbing things.

"Stop it," Xen pleaded with Owen. "I have a weak stomach."

Xen didn't need to remind us. Not only did he have a relaxed bladder, but he got hiccups whenever he was scared and gas when he was nervous, and we'd all witnessed various things that made him throw up. He once hurled after seeing a dirty cafeteria tray. Another time, an educational movie showing how to milk a cow made him toss his cookies. He even puked when one of our teachers was just talking about warm eggs.

I thought for sure he would blow chunks after seeing Owen bite into the large, wet blob, but Xen held it together and just hiccupped.

"It's pretty tasty," Owen reported. "I think it's Salisbury steak or something." He dipped his hand back into the can for more. As he pulled his fist out of the goo, a little something extra appeared.

Actually, a lot of something extra appeared.

Hundreds of wet spiders burst from the ooze and scurried up Owen's arm. Mindy screamed, and when Owen realized what was happening, he outscreamed Mindy by at least ten decibels, which is an above-average way of saying he almost burst my eardrums.

Owen whipped his hand from the ooze and flung spiders all over the small space. I dropped my phone and started to swat at the ones that had been flung onto me.

Xen started spewing chunks!

I could feel spiders biting me as I kept bumping up against my friends. Each time I jumped, my head hit the ceiling and I saw stars. I knocked over a puking Xen and tripped over Mindy.

I fell hard against the ooze-covered floor.

Owen bent over and charged at the back of the metal cabinet, pushing it out into the kitchen and creating an escape route. I scrambled up off my butt and followed Mindy through the opening. We all spazzed around, slapping and brushing off spiders like it was a choreographed dance.

I ran to one of the giant kitchen sinks and stuck my arms and face under the faucet. Mindy ran to another sink and climbed into it. She turned on the water and sat beneath it like she was taking a sink bath. All of us were hollering, and I felt certain that Nerf and his gang would hear us and return to the scene.

After a few uncomfortable minutes, we got ourselves brushed off and calmed down to a less hysterical mood. Owen whimpered as we each searched our arms and skin for bites. I had at least twenty welts. The others had slightly fewer.

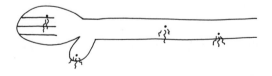

The marks didn't hurt so much, but they sizzled and were warm to the touch. The spiders who had followed us out or been flung off were now squished or hiding in the cafeteria somewhere.

"Eating school lunch in here seems more terrifying than ever," Xen said while shivering.

We pushed the cabinet back into place to hide the opening. I was pretty happy with the fact that we now had a secret place that most people in our school didn't know existed. In this day and age, anything secret was a bonus to survival. Of course our space had also been a source of ferocious canned spiders.

"I don't want to worry you guys," Owen said. "But I think I might have eaten a couple of spiders by accident."

"It's you who should be worried," I said. "Let's just hope they're not poisonous. Any idea what kind of spiders they were, Mindy?"

Mindy is an expert on all things bug. She likes them way more than any other person I know. She's the top student in our Bug Awareness class. Plus, she has an extensive worm-fly hybrid collection and also raises beetles in her beetle farm.

"I don't know exactly what kind of spiders those were,"

she admitted. "They looked like a steel-wolf spider variety, but they were covered in ooze."

Mindy crouched down and studied one of the flattened spiders on the ground.

"It's too smooshed to tell for sure," she reported. "Do you think they've been living in that can for thirty years?"

"Maybe they're some sort of arachnid that goes dormant," Xen suggested. "Arachnids that only come to life when a certain knucklehead bangs open their can with a rock and lets air in."

"Sorry," Owen whined.

In the distance, Finn the school crier began to cry out.

Four p.m. and all is done! Get home before the Fanatics fill the streets and all electricity is turned off. Also there was a red Windbreaker left on the bleachers. As is school law, it is now the property of Mrs. Susan. That is all!

I heard students outside the cafeteria exiting their classes and leaving the campus for the day. We decided to just go with Owen's plan and stay hidden in the kitchen and wait out the crowd. It would be much safer for us to leave after everyone was gone. While we were waiting, Principal Woth finally came slinking out of the pantry.

"Has everyone left for the day?" he asked.

"I think so," I answered. "Oh, and thanks for not ratting us out."

"I would have, if it got ugly," he said with a wink.

Principal Woth was spineless. He left the kitchen and vanished into the dark cafeteria. I took a minute to sigh out of frustration and all three of my friends did the same.

"This was a sucky day," I said needlessly. "It was supposed to be our day to make a point—Geeks united. Instead we were greased up, covered in paper, chased, bitten by angry spiders, and left to cower in the kitchen."

"Overall, not that surprising," Xen said.

"I agree with Xen," Owen said. "This is pretty much how our lives have been all year."

"You know tomorrow's not going to be any better,"

Mindy pointed out. "Everyone will still want to knock us down. Just because we got away today doesn't mean we're out of the woods."

"Mindy's right," Xen said. "I suggest we all go home and submit our names for attendance at some other middle school outpost. And then maybe, just maybe, one day we'll be able to live normal lives again."

I shivered as a strange and unfamiliar feeling ran down my spine through my legs and up my arms. My head suddenly felt heavy and started to throb like elfin drumbeats.

"I think I need to get home," I said seriously. "I don't feel so good."

The feeling rocked my body again. This time my fingers went numb and my toenails felt like they had low-voltage electricity buzzing beneath them.

"I . . ." My mouth locked up.

"Are you okay, Tip?" Mindy asked. "You don't look so good. Actually, I don't feel too well myself."

"Those spiders," Xen gasped. "They must have been poisonous!" He bent over and started to dry heave.

"That's not good," Owen said. He began to breathe hard.

"Maybe it wasn't spiders. Maybe it was that grease. It soaked into our skin, and now it's making us sick."

Xen hiccupped and farted at the same time. Normally he would have said "excuse me," but not today.

"What's happening?" I moaned.

"Must . . . get . . . out of here," Owen said as he bent over and held his stomach.

My arms and legs locked up. I felt like a skinny robot who had been rusted solid. None of us could move. Mindy tried to dial her phone while Owen moaned and Xen belched.

I heard Mindy saying something into her phone and then my body quivered and everything went black.

The last thing I remember was the sound of Owen retching.

CHAPTER NINE
The Awakening

I would have slept for many more hours if it hadn't been for the wet tongue of a wild suburban dog. Our city was filled with them and they often snuck into the school looking for food. One was now licking my face, and when I tried to shoo him away I realized there was more than one dog.

I sat up, panicked, and tried to figure out where I was. I definitely wasn't at home in my own bed. I was still in the dark kitchen surrounded by three sleeping Geeks and a dozen dogs who were licking our arms and faces.

"Get up!" I politely ordered my friends. "Mindy, Owen, Xen!"

All three began to stir and then scream as they realized that they were getting licked by stray dogs. I grabbed a broom next to one of the refrigerators and started shooing. Xen and Mindy joined me in the struggle, but Owen kept sleeping.

95

I stepped on his hand to gently let him know we needed his help.

We worked as a team to shoo the animals out of the kitchen. It wasn't that hard, since they all wanted to run off and look for something less combative to lick. Once they were gone, Xen asked, "Why are we still here?"

"The last thing I remember is feeling sick," I said.

"It's gotta be way past curfew," Owen said. "Why didn't anyone come looking for us?"

"I think I called my mom," Mindy said. "Maybe I told her I was having a sleepover. Actually I can't remember anything I said."

"Well, it definitely wasn't 'come and rescue us,'" I pointed out.

Because of government curfews, and Fanatics, and power outages, and, well, life, people can't always get home on time. I try to tell my parents where I am, but they know I'm a good hider and that I have sense enough to flee danger. Also, the government officials have said that nobody is worth looking for unless they've been missing for over a week.

"Wait," Mindy said. "Weren't we covered in spider bites before?"

"Splimp, I think I was."

We all looked at our arms and legs, and marveled at the fact that there were no longer any bite marks.

"Maybe we dreamed everything that happened today," Xen said. "I've had some really vivid dreams lately. I think it's because the government puts things in our milk."

"You get milk?" Owen asked jealously.

"Maybe we did dream everything," Mindy suggested. "Maybe we never filled that piñata with grease and the whole school still loves us. Wait, they never did."

"That's correct," Xen said. "And taking assessment of my odor, I can still smell trace amounts of grease. And dog drool."

"I smell nothing," Owen said while sniffing his right hand.

"Maybe we should all stop sniffing ourselves and get home," I suggested.

"But it's after curfew," Mindy reminded us. "We shouldn't be on the streets."

Like the rest of the country, the city of Piggsburg has an eight o'clock curfew. The government attempts to keep us safe. Also at eight, electricity is shut off, cars are not allowed on the roads, and packs of angry Fanatics take to the streets in large groups. The nighttime reminds them of when they first saw the horribly disappointing third movie. It's like every night is an anniversary of anger and disappointment. They hit the town in mad cliques that everyone else tries to avoid. Even the government has given up on the Fanatics. They've tried to stop them, but it always ends in riots. So the officials stay off the streets between eight and midnight and let the Fanatics work out their frustrations on their own. It might seem strange to the other places on earth, but we are under Marsha Law, and that's because the leader of the Fanatics in Piggsburg is a girl named Marsha Ledbetter.

She speaks only in emojis, and all Fanatics do whatever she does. She has millions of followers on social media. She is also the president of the Sand Throwers fan club. She was the first Fanatic to wear three bands on her leg. The bands represent the three books, and every true Fanatic now wears things in threes—three bands, three belts, three shirts. I've seen Marsha twice in person, and each time it was terrifying. I have no desire to go out into the neighborhood and accidentally run into her.

"So let's stay here at school," I said. "Mindy, can I use your phone to call my parents?"

"It's dead. Where's yours?"

We all looked at the metal cabinet that we had pushed back into place.

"I dropped it in there when I was running for my life."

"You have to get it," Xen said.

"I know I should. Just last week my dad lost his while the networks were down, and he tried texting by catapult."

I hope
they reply.

Cell phones are different these days. Before the collapse of everything, there was an overload of cell phones in the world. Some people had three of them, one for each hand and another to vibrate in their pocket to remind them they were popular. Since the world went wacko, most cities have tried to provide some spotty Wi-Fi so that people can still communicate. The Wi-Fi doesn't always work, but it's free. I got my phone three months ago. My dad traded a loaf of bread and a bike tire for it. It isn't a great phone, but I like it. It has some of my important notes about scientific formulas stored in it, as well as a few dirty jokes.

Knock knock.

Who's there?

Flaming bag of poo.

Flaming bag of poo, who?

Flaming bag of poo that'll soon be on your shoe.

And

What do you call a fish, a feather, and a fan?

I don't know, what?

F words.

Owen and Xen helped me move the pots and pans cabinet out from the wall. The three of us stared at the dark opening as if it was the portal to a very uneasy realm.

I suggested Owen go in and get my phone, but he declined.

"I'll do it," Mindy volunteered.

She walked into the dark and came out twenty seconds later with my phone.

It was dead, and since all the electricity was off for the night, there was no way for us to charge it.

"Let's get to my home so I can check in with my parents," I said. "Occasionally they wonder where I am."

We left the cafeteria and made our way through the

Goth section of WADD. Their area was in Z Hall, and it seemed more unsettling at night than it did during the day.

"It's a shame the Goths aren't here," I said. "They'd love how creepy this place is now."

WADD was even more dreary and dystopian-looking in the dark. The school was beat-up and in ill repair, and darkness made all the imperfections seem scarier.

"I think our school is plenty unsettling all the time," Owen said.

When we got to the security hole, it was wide open and unmanned. A cool steady breeze flowed in.

We quickly climbed out of the hole and ran across the street.

CHAPTER TEN

Attacked

Years ago, our neighborhood looked like the kind of place you'd see in a movie where kids were growing up with ordinary problems. But now it was completely different. Almost everyone had built walls around their homes or put up small guard towers on their roofs. People's lawns were overgrown and in disarray. There were a few houses where the owners tried to keep things groomed because they felt that even during a time of crisis they should still maintain a nice yard.

The problem with keeping things nice was that angry Fanatics, random thugs, or marauding animals never paid attention to where they were going. They would all trample lawns, gardens, anything that was in their way. Plus, people enjoyed shooting government drones down for sport. So yards were also littered with drone wreckage.

At the moment, Elm Street, the road in front of our school, was deserted.

"What time is it?" I asked Xen.

"Looking at the placement of the stars, it's eleven forty-seven," he answered.

We kept to the edges of the roads to hide among the shadows of trees and bushes. I continued to feel odd and more out of sorts than usual. My head felt heavy and then light again. My toes felt loose in my shoes. I kept glancing at my fingers to see if they were still attached to my hands.

"Does anyone else feel really strange?" I asked.

"I have my whole life," Owen replied.

When I explained what I meant, everyone admitted that they were also suffering similar symptoms. I wasn't sure, but something about those spider bites had changed me. As society had broken down, some animals and insects had started to act differently. A man on our block was bitten by a cat, and now the guy could only speak Chinese. Some blamed the extra radiation in the air from the drones. We didn't know what may have happened to the green goo in that tin can.

We came to a thick cement wall right next to a convenience store called Open When It's Safe. The store was small and it was only open when things seemed partially safe. It made all of us very uneasy to see that it was closed.

"Listen," I whispered as we stood with our backs pressed tightly against the cement wall. "We were bitten by spiders, right?"

Everyone nodded.

"And now we feel different," I went on. "I don't want to freak anyone out, but doesn't that remind you of someone?"

"Mr. Karl?" Xen asked.

Mr. Karl was the shop teacher. He had been bitten by a

wolf last year and had to have his leg amputated, which is a better-than-average way of saying it was chopped off.

"No," I said. "Spider-Man! He was bitten by a spider and then he had all kinds of superpowers. Maybe we have some sort of power now."

"I hope so," Owen said excitedly.

Owen turned around and attempted to climb the cement wall. When that didn't work, he tried to jump really high, but he couldn't get more than two inches off the ground.

"See if you can shoot web!" Xen said.

Owen held his arms out and tried as hard as he could to shoot webbing from his wrists. After a couple of minutes, he gave up and hung his head in disappointment.

"Try your butt," Xen suggested. "That's more like a real spider."

"Okay, maybe we're not Spider-Man," I conceded. "But something's happening to us."

"Yeah," Mindy agreed. "We're stuck out on the streets at midnight hoping to make it home without getting arrested or attacked and knowing that if we do actually get home, tomorrow is going to probably be worse than today. I just—"

"Hold on," Owen interrupted. "Someone's coming."

"What?" I asked. "There's no one around."

"I hear a big group of Fanatics."

"I don't hear anything," Mindy said. "And I have perfect hearing."

"Well, you might want to have it checked because they're on Bleak Street, two blocks over and about a mile to the east."

We all stared at Owen.

"Are you kidding?" I asked.

"Splimp, don't you guys know when I'm being serious? I can hear them."

"That's impossible," Mindy insisted.

"Actually"—Xen spoke up—"the human ear is capable

of discerning sound from miles away if the conditions are just right."

"Thanks, Xen," Mindy whispered sarcastically. "Everyone knows that."

"It's pretty late for Fanatics to be out en masse," I told Owen. "Are you sure?"

"Well, I'm telling you, it's a big group."

"And you think they're coming this way?" I asked.

"Yes."

"Then let's go," Mindy insisted. "Come on."

As Mindy said "come on," she clapped for emphasis. At that instant, one of the windows on the front of the Open When It's Safe store cracked, and the glass shattered with a terrifying noise.

We all ducked and screamed.

I looked up for a drone that might have dropped something, but the night sky was too dark to tell.

"Did someone throw a rock?" Xen asked.

"Um," Mindy whispered. "I think I might have done that."

Mindy clapped again and a second window on the front of the shop began to crack.

The glass popped and shattered. I covered my ears and closed my eyes as glass rained down on the sidewalk in front of the store. The bars over the windows were still in place, but the window glass was gone.

"That's incredible," I said.

"Superpowers!" Xen offered with excitement. "Positively out of this world. I wonder what I can do?"

Xen clapped a few times, but nothing happened. He put his hand to his ear to see if he could hear anything far away, but the disappointed look on his face made it clear that he couldn't. He tried to jump high, he tried to climb the wall, and he even tried to fly—all with no luck.

"Stop messing around, Xen," Owen scolded. "We need to keep moving before the Fanatics arrive."

"This stinks," Xen complained. "I was bitten as many times as you and Mindy."

"Let's worry about that later," Mindy said.

"Fine," Xen pouted. "If that's how it is. And so what? Breaking windows is not much of a superpower. It's probably just a coincidence. Or maybe someone threw a rock and broke it."

"What about Owen's hearing?" Mindy argued.

"Well, we're just taking his word for that," Xen said. "We don't know that he really heard anything."

"Um, maybe that will help you believe me."

Owen was pointing up Elm Street, to where a large group of girl Fanatics was marching down the road. As they got closer, we heard them chanting and hollering.

If they spotted us, they would talk or tear us to shreds—or post embarrassing pictures of us. I had been attacked before, and it wasn't fun.

We dashed around the side of the cement wall and past the store. I saw a large dumpster to hide in, but it was already occupied.

I considered waking the family, but I was raised to believe that bothering people (in dumpsters) late at night was a sign of bad manners. Next to the dumpster there was a parked car. I pulled open the front door and yelled, "Get in!"

We all scrambled into the beat-up car and locked the doors behind us. I was hoping no Fanatics had seen us, but the swarm was too smart and too observant. They surrounded the car and began pushing and banging against it from all sides while taking pictures and blinding us with their flashes.

"What do we do?" Owen hollered.

I felt around for any keys. Sure, I didn't have a license and it was illegal to be driving, but this was an emergency.

I searched everywhere near me, but there were no keys. I couldn't think straight due to all the Fanatics pounding on the car windows and taking flash pictures.

"Mindy, whatever you do, don't clap!" Xen yelled. "We need the windows to stay in place."

"I thought you said my gift wasn't real."

"It probably isn't, but just in case it is, don't test it now!"

More Fanatics swarmed the car. They began to rock the vehicle side to side, lifting it a little more with each shove. They were screaming about the Throwing Sand movie and how unfair life was while warning us that we were done for.

I took out my inhaler and inhaled like it was the end of the world—which it very well could have been. I tried to calm myself as I took stock of our situation. No matter how I viewed things, it didn't look good.

There were constant camera flashes going off. It looked like we were circled by a bright pulsing light. I could see some of the girls already posting the pictures. There was a good chance that my parents would see a picture of me taken moments before I died.

POSTED RIGHT THIS MOMENT

#EpicLifeFail

#SorryMomAndDad

#INeverGotToKissAGirl

I honked the horn but that just made them angrier. I was upset with myself for not paying more attention in Car Hacking class. I needed the dumb car to start. As I thought about it . . . it started!

"What happened?" Mindy screamed.

"I don't know," I yelled. "It just turned on!"

"Well, splimp, get us out of here!"

"But I don't know how to drive!"

"It's simple, really," Xen hollered. "Engage the car's gears by putting it into drive and step on the gas."

I did as I was instructed, and the car lurched slightly. The car's motion drove the already out-of-control Fanatics mad. I didn't want to run any of them over, but I also didn't want to die. I pressed lightly on the gas and the car began to roll forward. Some Fanatics moved out of the way, but one held on tightly to the roof.

I swerved carefully, and the poor Fanatic rolled off the roof and onto the grass. I flipped on the headlights, and Mindy honked the horn as I drove forward.

"Now!" Mindy shouted. "It's clear!"

As I pressed down on the gas, the car shot onto Elm Street. I turned as hard as I could to avoid hitting a tree, and the vehicle fishtailed.

I drove down Elm Street at lightning speed. At least I thought I was racing until Owen pointed out I was going only seventeen miles an hour. I guess it just felt fast because I had never driven before. I rocked up the speed to almost twenty-three miles an hour. The new velocity helped me easily outrun our assailants, which is an above-average way of saying they were Fanatics with a thirst for selfies.

I turned onto Oak Street and drove over a couple of lawns. Then I destroyed a few small bushes and wounded at least two mailboxes before I made it to my house. I pulled up onto the front lawn and the car shuddered to a stop. We all sat in silence for a few moments, trying to calm our beating hearts.

"That was way too close," Mindy said. "We're lucky you found the keys."

"Um . . . I didn't find any keys," I whispered. "I think I started the car with my mind. I just thought about it starting, and it did."

To test my theory, I imagined the vehicle starting up again, and instantly the motor revved to life. I thought of it turning off, and it shut down.

"No fair!" Xen complained. "I can't do anything!"

"Mind control?" Mindy said in awe. "Can you manipulate other things? I mean, can you levitate something?"

I imagined Mindy's backpack floating. It didn't move. I glanced at an old chair on my front lawn, but it didn't do a dang thing. I thought of the car starting up, and it did. One more thought, and the car turned off.

Owen and Xen were impressed—Mindy not so much.

"That's kind of an awkward superpower," she said.

"And clapping isn't? Let's just get inside my house before anything else attacks us."

The front door to my house was barricaded, but I shifted a few boards, and we climbed in. My parents were asleep. Obviously they thought I was somewhere else safely hiding.

"Can we sleep here?" Mindy asked. "I'm not walking home, and I don't want you driving me."

"Sure."

"Wait, maybe we should stay up and figure out what my gift is," Xen said.

"I think we should sleep on it," Owen said. "I'm pooped. Also, Tip, can I use your bathroom?"

Owen used the bathroom while Mindy, Xen, and I built a giant fort in the living room. A lot had happened in one day, and we were bushed. There was no use trying to stay awake to figure out what to do, or if Xen had a gift. Right now we needed sleep. Owen returned from the bathroom, and we all fell asleep feeling safe in our blanket-fortified fort.

CHAPTER ELEVEN

Important Origins

My dad is always the first one up in our house. He drives a supply truck on the edge of town for work. It's a dangerous job but only because he isn't a very good driver.

I had only four fender benders today.

While he was eating breakfast, he looked out the window and noticed the strange car on our lawn. His complaining about the car woke all of us up. We could hear him from the living room.

I thought I'd get in trouble, but because I usually do what I'm supposed to, my parents didn't even consider that

I could have been the one who parked a car on the lawn. I was a little bothered that they didn't think I was cool enough to do something like that.

My mom thought the car was probably left by someone who didn't have the money to fill the gas tank. Petrol was expensive, and sometimes it was just cheaper to abandon your vehicle on someone's lawn instead of filling up.

My mother stopped thinking about the car to complain to my father about her job at the Informant Hut at the mall. All day long, people would come in and tell on their friends and neighbors. My mom would then sell the information to the government and reward the people for being snitches. She hated everything about her job. But at least she had one.

"It's going to be crazy today," my mother said. "We're having a sale. Give us two secrets, and we'll pay for three."

"Maybe I'll stop by after work," my dad said. "I have a few things I could sell to you about my co-workers."

As much as I wasn't enjoying listening to my parents, I wanted to sleep. But I couldn't because my friends and I had to get going.

These days showing up late for school is not a good

thing. The government doesn't allow kids to miss any school unless they have a legitimate excuse.

My dog ate my homework, then he vomited it on an old lady, and I had to help her and give her an ounce of my blood. Plus, my hands are now tingling, and my vision is fading.

Life's hard. I'll text you your F.

If you have too many absences, they send you to Correction School, which is a big, ugly building behind our school where they force you to earn extra credit by breaking up old concrete for the gravel factories.

"We can't be late," I said urgently as I nudged Xen.

"You know Nerf's still going to mess with us," Xen pointed out.

"That's a splimp of a lot better than cracking gravel."

All four of us crawled out of our blanket fort.

"Wait," Mindy asked. "Did I dream that we had some weird abilities last night? Or was that real?"

"It was real," Xen complained. "You guys can do freaky things, but not me."

Sleep had made me forget about the spiders and the fact that I could start a car with my thoughts. I imagined the vehicle in the front yard turning on, and we all heard it come to life. My father ran outside with his assault shovel to see what was happening.

"Try starting something else," Mindy suggested.

I looked around and spotted our beat-up microwave in the kitchen. I thought of it being on and just like that, it came to life and began humming.

"Pretty cool," Owen said enviously. "You can heat up burritos from across the room. By the way, I can still hear really well. I can hear Darth Susan at school. She's yelling at some kid for showing up without a shirt on."

"You can hear *that* far away? It's like miles."

"I can hear what I want to hear and shut out what I want to shut out. Like, right now at my house, my mom is telling

123

my dad about how bad my grades are. She's also talking about how much trouble I'm going to be in for not coming home last night. I think I'll stop listening now."

"I guess I'm not that jealous of your gift," Xen said.

We stopped talking and took turns washing up in the laundry room sink. Then we had a fast breakfast of wheat and stale marshmallows. Good food wasn't easy to come by. In the olden days, my mom would go grocery shopping and come home with all kinds of amazing things—frozen meals, sandwich stuff, fruits and vegetables. Now, whenever she goes shopping, she has to fight for whatever she can get her hands on, and it's never anything delicious.

I got canned pig's feet, lumpy pie filling, irregular peas, and misshapen circus peanuts.

The government doesn't do much to help. They actually made things worse by creating their lousy food parallelogram to let us know what we should be eating.

FOOD PARALLELOGRAM

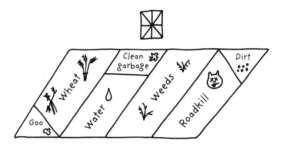

With our stomachs full of wheat, marshmallows, and worry, we headed back to the place where we knew we'd still be in trouble—school.

The streets were clear this morning, and there was a blood-moon sun with slight ash in the air. Owen heard a group of angry men three streets over, but they were nothing to worry about because they were heading in the opposite direction from us.

Carefully we made our way over to Otto Waddle Jr. High Government Outpost. We moved between trees and houses and crouched behind bushes and burned-out cars. Owen's ability to hear far away was super helpful, but he was struggling with hearing us close up.

When we were a few blocks away from WADD Xen spotted a car coming down the road and Owen listened in. He heard Nerf bragging about his driving skills and talking about how good he looked in a tank top.

I couldn't believe it. Nerf was driving? It was against the law for him to be behind the wheel. Sure, I had done a little driving last night, but that was an emergency and in the dark. Nerf was too young. Besides, driving in the daylight was forbidden unless people were going to and from work.

Dashing across the street, we crouched down behind some overgrown bushes. Through the leaves I focused my mind on the car Nerf was driving, and just like that, his engine turned off. The vehicle rolled to a stop in the middle of Elm Street.

Owen was the only one with amazing ears, but we could all hear Nerf swearing now. He hopped out of the car with Mud and Weasel and a couple of other Jocks.

Help me push the car off the road. If the government finds it, they'll notify my parents. And if my parents find out, I'm dead.

If you die, can I have your shoes?

Keeping hidden, we continued toward the school. I was happy about my new ability. There's never been anything special about me, but now I was like a psychic key that could turn things on and off.

We got in the security hole and walked down Q Hall without anyone giving us grief. In fact, people seemed to be ignoring us as we walked through the school. One of the Goths had a perfect chance to make fun of me when I tripped and hit the water fountain, but he said nothing.

In first hour, no one laughed at my hair or hit me with spit wads. I couldn't figure out what was happening. Maybe things were different today. Maybe what we had tried to do yesterday had secretly inspired the masses to stand up for themselves. Maybe we were some sort of heroes everyone now respected.

In my second-hour Pop Culture History class, I sat in my desk at the back of the room as the teacher droned on and on about the history of movies.

Now, *Paul Blart, Mall Cop, Number Twelve, Blart Farts,* that was a masterpiece.

Nobody said anything to me in that class either. Usually by this time in the day, I had been made fun of or bothered a few times. But it was as if I was invisible. A thought struck me.

Hey, Tip, maybe you're invisible.

It was possible. I mean I can start and stop things. Maybe those spider bites gave me the gift of invisibility as well. My spine tingled. I stuck my hands up in the air like I was asking two questions at one time. My teacher didn't notice. I stood up and said,

Nobody did! I couldn't believe it! My whole life I had dreamed of being invisible, and now it seemed like my dream had come true. I did a little dance and shook my butt at a member of the Dark Arts.

"Um, are you feeling okay, Tip?" he asked.

Apparently I wasn't invisible after all.

I sat down as quickly as I could.

My face burned, and everyone laughed. I wasn't invisible, just being ignored.

In my next hour class I wasn't bothered again. I felt a bit let down. Yesterday the AV Club had done something really stupid and now nobody was giving us any credit.

At lunchtime my friends and I met behind the school in the burned-out shed. All of us had been left alone—not a single wedgie or pantsing to mention.

"Someone even held the door open for me," Mindy said.

"Maybe they know we have powers," I suggested.

"Right. You mean maybe they know *you* have powers," Xen said, still pouting over his lack of spider-bite abilities.

Xen would have gone on complaining, but we heard talking just outside the shed. We all snuck out and peeked around the corner to spy.

Standing near the back of the school was a Goth student named Rick. He had wandered away from his group and was now being picked on by Nerf and his friends. It was a jam I had been in more times than I cared to count. And every time something like that happened, not a single person came to my rescue. I felt horrible for Rick, but there was nothing we could—

"Wait a second," I whispered. "We could help Rick."

"What?" Owen asked.

"Mindy," I said with excitement, "do you think you can clap out one of the windows on the back of the school? That might scare Nerf into stopping."

"I can try," Mindy replied.

Nerf was standing next to a small window. He had his back to the glass, and Rick was shaking nervously in front of him.

Mindy reached out her arms and clapped twice.

The window didn't break, but a flagpole nearby cracked at the base and came toppling down toward Nerf. He reached up to grab the falling pole, but it struck his shoulder and knocked him to the ground. Nerf's friends just stood there looking as dense as they were while their leader struggled and whined from beneath the pole. He was okay. More humiliated than anything, I think.

For once Nerf truly looked like a log.

Rick took off as fast as he could, and we ran back into the burned-out shed.

"That was—" Owen started to say.

"Awesome," I finished for him.

"I thought I could break glass, not poles."

"You know what this means?" I asked. "We're not just Geeks anymore. The grease piñata was a bust, but think of what we can do now. It's like we're a group of superheroes."

"Great," Xen complained. "So where does that leave me?"

"You can be the manager," Mindy suggested. "You know, keep us organized."

"What?" Owen asked Mindy.

"I said, he can be the manager!"

"We could use that hidden room in the kitchen as our headquarters," I said. "Like a Geek Cave."

"Well then, as manager I think our first job should be to make sure all the spiders are gone."

"And we'll need a name," Owen said. "How about the League of Amazing and Magnificent Entities?"

We all stared at Owen.

"I like the word *entities*," he said sheepishly.

"No offense," Xen said, "but as manager I think I should

point out that your new abilities aren't really that amazing or magnificent."

"Fine," I said. "Then how about League of Average and Mediocre Entities instead?"

"You realize the acronym is LAME," Xen pointed out.

"That sort of fits us."

"Yeah," Mindy agreed. "Plus, it's under the radar and not too showy."

"What?" Owen asked.

"We're going with your suggestion," I told Owen. "LAME it is."

"Just remember," Xen said. "With average power comes average responsibility."

Mindy moaned.

"Sorry," Xen apologized. "I just felt like one of us had to say that."

"Okay then, we'll be Geeks by day and LAME by night," I cheered.

"Actually, it's midday now," Xen pointed out. "And we just took care of our first caper."

"Okay, okay," I said. "We'll be Geeks by day and LAME continually. Or at least when we need to be."

I stuck my hand out, and the other three did the same.

I don't know what it was. Maybe it was the fact that we had all been bitten by spiders just yesterday. Or maybe it was because we were hopped up on Nerf getting a little flagpole payback. Or maybe it was because the wheat and marshmallows weren't sitting that well with me. Whatever it was, I felt weird. Not a bad weird, just odd. Like something big was finally happening in my life.

Finn the crier cried out.

Lunchtime is over.
Stop feeding your face.
Also, there is a strange
glow coming from the
language arts building!

The four of us obediently headed back. All the other students at WADD had no idea of what a momentous event had just happened in the burned-out shed behind the school. LAME had been born, and because of that, justice was going to be served.

CHAPTER TWELVE

The Threat

It might seem kind of lame to be excited about LAME, but I was. I could barely think of anything else the rest of the day. During classes, I tried sketching out potential costumes for myself and worked on coming up with a name.

I was still a little confused as to why nobody was giving us grief about the grease incident—nothing, not a Wet Willie, or a Slappy Sam, or even a Punch Hug.

At the beginning of our last class, AntiSocial Studies, a girl named Cindy Fargus turned around and looked at me. She was a part-time Fanatic, which meant she terrorized the streets on weekends, but she was still working toward her education during the week. She had never glanced at me before.

"You smell like grease," she said.

"Thank you?"

Cindy turned back around. She was right. I hadn't taken a shower this morning. Yes, I had washed my face, but my arms still stank.

I took out a piece of mint gum and rubbed it under my armpits. It was a trick I had learned from watching a No-Privacy-for-YouTube video about deodorant life hacks.

Halfway through AntiSocial Studies, the intercom came to life with a loud crackle. The crackle was followed by the sticky-sweet voice of Darth Susan. I wanted to ignore her, but she was talking about the AV Club.

Attention, Geeks!
I need Tip, Owen, Mindy, and Xennitopher to report to my office immediately.

Everyone around me gulped.

It was never a good thing to be summoned by Darth Susan. It usually meant Correction School or weeding or worse—she'd make you climb up the tower and empty Finn's toilet bucket.

Everyone was silent as we left the classroom. They knew there was nothing they could say to us that would make us feel worse than we already did. We had almost survived the day, but now we were doomed.

Besides Becky, the hall monitor lizard, there was nobody in sight. Becky roamed the halls nipping at people's ankles to make sure everyone was in class. Darth Susan let Becky out during class time and took her home with her at night. Becky was her beloved pet.

Who's my widdle wovely lizard? Are you my scaly baby? Yes you are.

Every student at WADD hated Becky. She made our school even more miserable than it already was. She also pooped wherever she wanted and tracked it all over. I don't know if you're familiar with lizard poop, but it's disgusting. It's also no fun to find it on top of your desk or in your gym shoes.

At the moment, Becky was eating a sweater someone had foolishly left in their locker. The smelly lizard didn't pay attention to us as we tiptoed down the hall toward the office.

"So what do you think Darth Susan wants from us?" I whispered.

"I . . . don't . . . know," Xen said, beginning to hiccup.

Owen listened to see if he could hear what she was up to. But she wasn't making any noise.

We walked down Q Hall feeling like inmates on death row.

I could see no way for us to get out of this. We had messed up yesterday and now we were going to have to pay the price.

"Should we notify our parents of our impending death?" Owen asked.

"Mindy could clap at Darth Susan," Xen suggested. "Maybe she'll fall apart."

When we got to the office Darth Susan was behind her desk high on her throne. She smiled down at all of us and then asked us to sign our names in the office logbook. Darth Susan was not only horrible, but she was organized and loved to do all the little things that made her office feel like a real school office. After we had signed in, she looked down at us and sighed.

"Such troublemakers," she said. "Principal Woth is very concerned about you four. He feels you're disrupting the learning of the other WADD students."

"He does?" I asked, surprised that Principal Woth had any opinion of us at all.

"Well, I can't be sure," she continued, "seeing how the principal and I rarely speak. He's a busy man, running the school from wherever he's hiding. The point is I have something I need the four of you to do."

"What is it?" Owen asked.

"Tomorrow, as you know, the school will be taking the SLAP."

Of course we knew about the SLAP: Finn had been crying about it for weeks. It was a nationwide test that the government made all students take. SLAP stood for Stop Learning and Panic. So all Staffers were forced to stop teaching for a day and start worrying about how we'd do.

Depending on the school's test performance, the school could get more supplies and money.

Everyone except us Geeks hated the test—for us it was a chance to show off. Of course we never got credit for doing well; in fact we were never even told our scores. Maybe that was why we'd been called in. Maybe we weren't in trouble, and she just wanted to give us an award. Maybe we were finally going to get the credit we deserved. Or maybe monkeys were going to fly down from the sky out of cloud butts and start handing everyone money and food.

Actually, the monkey thing seemed more likely to happen than Darth Susan being nice to us.

"Do you know why you're here?" she asked.

"Body odor?" Owen guessed. " 'Cause I didn't take a shower last night."

Darth Susan shook her head in disgust. She looked like my mom when my dad told her that we were out of toilet paper and would have to start using leaves again.

"You're not here because of body odor," she said sweetly. "If that was the problem, the whole school would be on lockdown. You're here because tomorrow is the SLAP, and last year the four of you got perfect scores, the highest in the district."

"Thank you," Mindy said, blushing.

"I don't want a thank-you," Darth Susan snapped. "I brought you here to make sure it doesn't happen again."

Most of the time, high scores are good. Even in our messed-up society, a lot of people still want good grades. The government is always going on and on about how important it is for us to be smarter than the rest of the world. And getting good grades is what we Geeks excel at. As the AV Club, all we do is push carts around and deliver projectors and electricity pods. Sometimes we set up microphones or are in charge of the spotlight during the lice patrol.

Doing well on tests—that is definitely our thing.

"You don't want us to do well on the test?" I asked Darth Susan.

"Actually, I insist that you fail."

"I don't understand."

"That's the spirit, Xen," she said with a smile. "Just keep playing dumb."

My school never ceased to disturb me.

Darth Susan explained that, for the sake of our school, we had to fail the test. Last year she had kept our four tests and not turned them in to the district. She had even taken them home and burned them to destroy all evidence. But this time the District Compound was sending an official Pep Liaison to administer the test and make sure every student took it.

"What's a Pep Liaison?" Xen asked Darth Susan.

"Annoying" was her only answer.

I knew what a Pep Liaison was. For fun last summer I had studied the government's book of officials—now I knew everyone, from the Drone Mayor to the Vice President of Chaos. The Pep Liaison worked at the District Compound and was in charge of making sure all schools acted happy, even when times were bad, which was all the time. He also made sure students were taking the SLAP and that they weren't complaining or cheating.

I guess the country was having a real problem with people cheating in all seventy-three states. Schools desperately wanted to get extra funding from the government of the Somewhat United, Sort of Divided States of America, also known as the SUSDSA.

According to Darth Susan most schools weren't cheating to make themselves look better, they were cheating to make themselves look worse. The low-scoring schools got most of the funds. They also got tons of extras, like fireproof desks and attack-proof port-a-potties.

I used to think that Otto Waddle Jr. High Government Outpost was above cheating. I also used to think that expired milk wouldn't give you the slipperies.

Darth Susan had more to say. "WADD wouldn't have the supplies we now have if the district had seen your scores last year. So you all must fail this test."

"But—" I tried to say.

"No butts, rears, or derrieres," she insisted. "Tomorrow's test is the most important one in the history of this school. The reward for the lowest score is going to be ours. Do you understand?"

All four of us stared at her.

"Let me ask you something," she continued. "Why do you think everyone ignored you today?"

We kept staring.

"A day after you made fools of yourselves in front of the whole school, and nobody's picking on you. Who do you think made that happen?"

More staring.

"I'll tell you—it's because I instructed every Staffer to make sure you're left alone. They've let every student know that, for the moment, you're off-limits. And if you fail the test like good children, then you'll remain off-limits. But, if you decide to be troublemakers and do your best, then I'm afraid I can't be responsible for how people treat you. Understand? Passing is bad; failing is good."

I could see that Mindy was holding her hands together and fighting the urge to clap at Mrs. Susan.

"I'll take your silence as a yes. Now just come to school tomorrow prepared to be losers."

We left her office and stepped into the hall. Owen was the first to speak up.

"I wonder what kind of supplies the lowest school gets this year. I mean, splimp! They must be incredible for Darth Susan to try to bribe us."

"Yeah," Xen said. "We should find out."

"That sounds like the perfect first case for LAME," I whispered. "After class, let's meet at the Geek Cave."

"What if the spiders are still in there?" Xen asked.

"I'll borrow a flamethrower from shop class," Owen volunteered. "If there are any left, that'll clear them all out."

Becky the lizard spotted us and began to gallop in our direction. She was looking for some ankles to bite and had some feces, which is an above-average way of saying poop, to share.

"Move!" I shouted.

We all began to run.

The running probably wasn't necessary. Becky had spotted some Loners loitering at the end of Q Hall, and she was already moving away from us to monitor the situation.

CHAPTER THIRTEEN

Branded

After school we headed to the dark and sticky cafeteria. There were a few Goths hanging around the entrance, but we got rid of them by saying there was a sale on black nail polish down at Wargreens. They took off as fast as they could while still looking mopey.

We walked through the empty cafeteria and hopped over the counter into the kitchen. Owen had not been able to borrow a flamethrower, but he did have a small torch. Once we were standing in front of the pots and pans cabinet, he lit the torch, and me and Xen moved the cabinet out from the wall.

The Geek Cave looked particularly dark.

"Who's checking for spiders?" I asked.

"I suggest that Owen does," Xen said. "Since he's already holding the torch."

"You can hold it." Owen tried to hand it to Xen.

"Here," Mindy said.

She grabbed the torch and bent down to scoot into the room.

"It's all clear," she yelled back. "No spiders!"

The rest of us bravely crawled in.

The torch lit the Geek Cave nicely. I'd been worried that we would be smoked out, but there was a vent in the low ceiling that allowed all the smoke from the flame to evacuate the room. The three empty tin cans were still there, and the fourth one that had contained the goo was now empty as well. Whatever had been in the can and splashed on the floor was gone. It had either been eaten by mice or it had evaporated, which is an above-average way of saying something in a way that Nerf and his friends don't understand.

We set up the four large tin cans, and each of us took a seat on one.

There was a lot for us to think about, but most importantly we needed to figure out what the reward was for our school failing the SLAP. That meant LAME would have to sneak into Darth Susan's office.

It took some thinking, but we finally decided on a plan of action. First, we would leave the Geek Cave. Second, Owen would listen for trouble as we approached the office. Third, when we reached the office, Mindy would clap the door hinges open. And fourth, I would climb up to Darth Susan's desk and use my ability to start her computer.

Hopefully there would be information there that told us what the school would get and why she so desperately wanted WADD to fail the test.

To be honest, there was a part of me that thought it might be best to just go ahead and fail the test. I really liked it when the school ignored us. It made for a much more enjoyable learning environment. Not a single person had bothered me that day. Even Nerf pretended I wasn't there.

We hunkered down in the dark room until everyone had cleared out of the school for the day. It was a known fact that Darth Susan didn't like to stay around when the day was over. She liked to leave the instant Finn cried out.

School's over for the day. There's an uncomfortable fog rolling through the halls. Get out while you can!

She claims that she must leave quickly because Becky needs to get home to feed. But we all know that she really wants to get as far away from us as possible and as fast as she can. Darth Susan dislikes us almost as much as we dislike her. She's always talking about retirement and wishing she could be done with us.

With WADD finally empty, we snuck through the halls. Each of us took turns asking Owen if he could hear anything. His answer was always the same.

"What?"

Near the end of Z Hall, Owen held his arm out to stop us and whispered, "There's someone around the corner."

We ducked behind the closest book barrier and held our breath.

Book barriers are made up of old books that nobody reads. The books are nailed and stapled together to form a big pile. People use them to hide from enemies or surprise government inspectors, or for protection from anything that might be flying through the air.

We tried to see who Owen had heard, but there was no one. Thirty seconds later, Tyler the janitor came walking down the hall. He was pushing a broom and tracking mud all over the floor with his dirty shoes.

Nobody was supposed to hang around after school. If caught, we'd be kicked out or Tyler would make us help him clean. Either way, our plan would be spoiled.

My heart was beating a million miles a minute. Which I know is an inaccurate and impossible thing for a heart to do, but the moment called for a little dramatic embellishment. I could hear Owen sweating, because he makes a low crackly noise when he does.

"Splimp, I'm sweating like a sun orc," he whispered.

"Actually," Xen corrected Owen, "sun orcs don't sweat—they drip."

I wanted to point out that they were both wrong. Everyone knows that the sun orcs from the Orc in the Road graphic novels don't sweat or drip; they leak. But there wasn't time to argue about things like that right now.

Tyler stopped and swiveled his trash-can-covered head. He looked around the hall, shrugged, and then kept on walking. Either he hadn't seen us, or he had seen us and just didn't care. We all stayed behind the barrier for a couple of minutes until we were sure the coast was clear.

Once everything was silent, we slipped out from behind the barrier and started walking toward the office.

"Wait," Xen said. "While we were cowering behind those books, I drew up a quick logo for our group."

"What?" Mindy asked.

"As manager, I feel we need a logo. It's called branding."

"Don't you think we should talk about that later?" I whispered.

Xen looked hurt.

"Fine," I apologized.

We all stopped walking and took a quick look at what Xen had drawn.

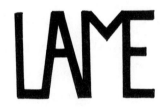

"I like it," Mindy said.

"Yeah, it's really good," I agreed. "Now, can we go?"

"Thanks," Xen replied. "I just think things will be more official now that we have a logo."

The four of us, plus our logo, set off to complete our quest.

CHAPTER FOURTEEN
Hiding for a Cause

The door to Darth Susan's office was locked. Mindy clapped her hands near the door's hinges, and the doorknob cracked and then fell off. It wasn't what Mindy meant to do, but it worked. It was dark inside the office, but we couldn't risk turning on the lights. Now I just needed to climb up the desk throne to Darth Susan's desk.

Good luck, Tip.

"Luck is an abstract concept that only simpleminded people believe in," I whispered back.

"That's what I meant," Mindy added.

I'm not positive here, but I think we were flirting.

I began scaling the desks, knowing that if anyone found us, I would be the one in the most trouble. After all, I was on top of Mrs. Susan's sacred pile of desks. We were forbidden to touch her stuff, let alone climb it.

When I got to the top, I stopped to take a look at the view. I could see the dark forms of my friends down below, and it finally made sense to me why Darth Susan sat up so high. I felt powerful and better than all the little people beneath me.

"It's pretty cool up here," I whispered loudly.

"Stop looking down at us and start snooping," Xen whispered loudly back.

I pulled open the desk drawers to see if there were any clues, but they were just filled with a bunch of the supplies Darth Susan was hoarding. I was tempted to swipe a few pens and a roll of toilet paper, but I didn't think that was something a superhero should do.

Darth Susan's computer required a government-issued key to start it. Luckily, all I had to do was think about her computer being on and it flashed to life. Still, it required a password to open the files. My friends offered up their suggestions.

"Selfish1."

"LizardLover."

"Born2BAwful."

I appreciated the suggestions, but I decided to try one of my own.

IH8KIDS

It worked. I sat down on her desk chair and started typing.

Darth Susan had a number of files and folders on her computer's desktop screen. One folder was labeled LIZARD FACTS, and another contained the instructions for making your own beetle jerky. There was one that said PALS and another that said SCHOOL ATTENDANCE RECORDS. There were a lot of files, but I couldn't see any for the SLAP test.

"Anything?" Mindy asked.

"No," I replied. "There isn't . . . Wait a second. Darth Susan doesn't have any pals."

I should have known—*pals* spelled backward is *slap*. I opened the file, and instantly I saw why she wanted us to fail the test.

This was big!

I pressed Print, and a printer one desk down spit out a piece of paper. As the paper slipped out onto the tray, Owen spoke up.

"Tip, there's someone in the hall, and they're headed this way."

"Who is—"

Before I could get the words out of my mouth, Owen whispered loudly, "Hide!"

I saw the dark silhouettes of Mindy, Xen, and Owen disappear beneath the bottom desks. I used my mind to turn off the computer, and I grabbed the piece of paper from the printer. Then, as quickly as I could, I crawled under Darth Susan's desk.

The office door opened, and through a small crack, I saw Darth Susan enter the room.

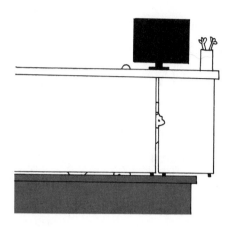

She turned on the light and stared at the broken door-knob that was now in her hand.

"What happened?" she asked, her voice sounding both sweet and suspicious. "Doorknobs don't just break."

"Yes they do," a smiling man said. He was standing next to her and wearing a sash across his government uniform that said PEP LIAISON. "There are so many broken things in society these days. But then again, there are so many things that aren't. Now, do you have that tape you promised me?"

Darth Susan looked around the office and glanced up at her desk. I didn't know what to do, and as I was wishing that the lights would go off, they went off.

"Flat moldy noodles," Darth Susan said.

She flipped the switch a couple of times, and the lights came back on. I quickly turned them off again.

"The electricity in this town is pathetic," she complained. "President Flake should be punished for the way he runs our government."

Careful how you talk about Flake. He is our leader and my distant sixth cousin twice removed and half bonkers.

"Right," Darth Susan said. "Some leader."

"Don't fret, I have a torch." Mr. Pep struck a match and lit a torch to light the office. "I always carry a spare. You can't be too careful these days."

"You smile too much," Darth Susan said.

Using the firelight, she began scaling the desks. For an older woman, she was a pretty good climber. She scrambled up faster than I had, and she was seconds away from finding me. Through the crack I looked for anything else in the office I could turn on or off. I spotted an old radio on one of the bottom desks and thought it on.

The world is going to end,
but you're still my best friend.
So . . . let me call you sweetie, sweetie.
I think that you're sweet.
Let me call you neaty, neaty.
The whole world thinks you're neat.
Even though we're all dead meat.

Darth Susan heard the music and temporarily stopped climbing. She growled and began to bark at the Pep Liaison.

"Did you turn that radio on?"

"No," he replied, "but I do love this song."

"Turn it off," she yelled.

The Pep Liaison turned off the radio, and since I hated the song that was playing, I decided to leave it that way.

"What's going on here?" Darth Susan muttered as she got to her desk and stood behind it. "Something is askew."

I actually agreed. Things were askew, which is an above-average way of saying things were out of place. I was out of place and under her desk. And because I was out of place, I could see her feet and knees. I wondered why my friends weren't somehow trying to help me.

Darth Susan sat down at her desk chair and scooted in. Her knees were now less than an inch away from me. She shifted in her chair, and just as she started to scoot in farther, I heard a cracking noise and watched her drop away from her desk. She let go of the torch and fell down onto the next row of desks. With a sloppy roll, she bounced off those desks and all the way to the ground. I could barely see through the crack where she landed. But I could hear her whimpering. The Pep Liaison ran to her.

"My goodness, what a fall," he said. "You forget about the tape. Let's get you someplace comfortable."

Mr. Pep helped Darth Susan to her feet and the two of them left, shutting the door behind them. I waited at least a full minute before exhaling. I waited five more before I stuck my head out from under the desk and whispered down.

"Are you guys okay?"

"I think so," Mindy whispered back. "I clapped softly to break the ceiling light."

"But you broke her chair instead."

"As manager of this league, I feel the need to remind all of you that your abilities seem a bit daft," Xen said.

"But I can turn lights on and off now," I bragged. "That's something."

"I guess," Xen muttered.

I climbed out from beneath the desk and worked my way down to ground level. I waved the piece of printed paper with the information from Darth Susan's computer.

Everyone stared at the paper, but it was too dark to see. Before I could even think about switching the lights back on, Mindy tapped on her phone's flashlight.

"Thanks, Mindy."

"For what?"

"For the light."

"I didn't turn on the light."

I looked up from the paper and yelped. Owen's eyes were burning like two small lightbulbs.

Owen closed his eyes, and the room went dark. He opened them again and we all saw the light.

"Whoa," Mindy whispered.

"Not fair," Xen said with a growl. "Not fair at all. You have multiple gifts and I have none."

Owen looked around the room. The light from his eyes swept the space like small spotlights.

"That's pretty cool," I admitted. "Does it help you see really far away? Or can you look through things?"

"Nope," Owen said. "In fact everything's kind of blurry."

Owen shone his eyes onto the paper and we all read.

> If Otto Waddle Jr. High Government Outpost fails one more time, it will be permanently shut down, and all students will be shipped to outpost #72.

"Darth Susan doesn't want us to fail the test so we can get more supplies," I said. "She wants us to fail so that the school will be shut down forever and she can retire early and with disaster benefits."

"We can't let that happen," Mindy insisted. "WADD's not perfect, but I've heard real horror stories about outpost #72."

All four of us shuddered.

Outpost #72 was not a good place. It was on the edge of Piggsburg, and bad things happened there. It was where the government sent all of its problem students and some minor criminals. Students were constantly getting hurt by some of the social networking gangs that ruled its halls.

"We've got to pass that test," I said. "We have to make sure that the Pep Liaison delivers our scores to the District Compound tomorrow after school."

"How are we going to do that?" Owen asked.

I thought for a moment before I spoke.

"I might have some ideas. Who here likes to sew?"

All three of my friends raised their hands. I should have remembered that we had gotten As in our Survival Sewing and Knitting class.

"All right, we need to get to my house," I insisted. "It's time to sew and think about a few things."

We crawled through the security hole without trouble. And besides a stray dog trying to steal Owen's shoe and a light acid rain shower, we made it home safely.

Once at my house, we all went straight to work.

CHAPTER FIFTEEN

Betrayed

My friends got permission from their parents to sleep over this time. The four of us were up almost all night working on our projects.

After we finished, we got a few hours of sleep in the blanket fort before we had to get up and head back to WADD.

Good morning, Xen.

Good morning, Owen.

Good morning, Tip?

I hope so, Mindy.

When we got to school, there was a line at the security hole, but eventually we made it through without any problem. If our school had had an X-ray machine, like the high school did, the guards at the security hole might have noticed that under our clothes we were wearing some very unusual outfits.

We were prepared to do whatever we could to pass the test and get our scores to the District Compound.

After the morning announcements from Darth Susan, all of us students were marched into the auditorium by government officials and told to take our seats.

We were then forced to listen to the Pep Liaison blather and blather, which is a better-than-average way of saying he bored the snot out of us.

The very integrity of your school depends on how well you do on this test. The world may be falling apart, but keep calm and test on! As Pep Liaison of Piggsburg, I demand that you smile and do your best!

After he was done, the SLAP tests were passed out by Staffers. The Pep Liaison honked a bike horn to officially start the test.

Sadly, WADD was home to a good number of students who were kind of dolt-like. Also nobody cared about doing well. The Goths hated tests, the Sox couldn't hold pencils correctly, the book-loving Pens just liked to read the test, and the Jocks used the paper to floss their teeth. Sure, there was always the possibility that someone besides us would rise to the occasion and do their best, but there was a better possibility that only us Geeks would even *complete* the SLAP.

At noon, Lunch Lady Sniddle served us rubbery carrots and canned tuna, and we had to eat it while taking the test. A couple of students got tuna juice on their tests, so they had to start over.

By the end of last period, my head hurt and I was sweaty—it didn't help that I was secretly wearing more than one outfit.

The Pep Liaison honked the bike horn, letting us know that the test time was over. I filled in the last answer quickly.

We all lined up and handed in our tests to Mr. Peppy.

"And remember," he said as he took each test. "You're never fully dressed without a smile, which means when you frown, you're half naked."

Finn screamed out.

The day is over! Exit as quickly as possible or the sun may not come out tomorrow. Also, to the owner of the burning car in the Staffers' parking lot, you left your lights on.

Everyone left the auditorium and made their way off campus. We Geeks snuck into the cafeteria and headed straight to the Geek Cave.

Owen moved the pots and pans cabinet, and we slipped inside.

The darkness caused Owen's eyes to glow and light up

the secret room. Fortunately, there was still no sign of bugs. It's tough being a superhero when you're scared of spiders.

Xen pulled the cabinet closed, and we all took off our top clothes to reveal the costumes we had stitched last night.

Together we were LAME. We were also nervous, but there was no time to be scared. We had something we needed to take care of.

"We should probably find out what kind of spiders those were that bit us," Mindy said. "It might help us better understand our powers."

"If we live, that's a good idea," I said.

"If we live?" Owen asked.

"No time for fear," Xen insisted. "Do your thing, Owen."

Owen tilted his head and lifted his right ear up. He could hear Darth Susan telling some kids to leave her office, followed by the sound of her kissing Becky.

"Eww," Xen said. "Nobody told me this mission would be repulsive."

"Sorry. Wait, I can hear the Pep Liaison coming into the office. He's telling Darth Susan how the test went off without a hitch and that he has all the tests in his bag. Once he turns them into the District Compound, they will be tallied, and the results will be final."

"What else?" Mindy asked.

"Darth Susan just told him good job, and Peppy said thanks."

"Your hearing really is impressive," Mindy said.

Owen didn't hear her, but he continued to repeat what Darth Susan and the Pep Liaison were saying.

"Darth Susan just asked Peppy for our four tests so that she can take them home and burn them. I guess she didn't trust us to fail. Now he just told her that he'll hand over the tests when she hands over the tape."

"He's going to give her the tests?" I asked in shock. "So the Pep Liaison's bad?"

"I can't believe it," Xen said. "He always seems so happy."

"There must be something really awful on that tape he wants," Mindy said. "Maybe it's some footage of him frowning."

"I don't know what it is, but if our tests don't get turned in, it's outpost #72 for all of us."

Owen continued to repeat what he heard: "Darth Susan just gave him the tape, and it's not a videotape—it's three rolls of Scotch tape. He's saying that he needs it for scrapbooking."

"What?" Mindy complained. "He's selling us out for Scotch tape?"

"Scrapbooking can be addictive," Xen said.

"Forget about the tape," I insisted. "What else is he saying?"

"He gave her our four tests, and now she's informing him that she wants Nerf and his goons to escort him to the District Compound. That way she can make sure things go right."

"This is bad," Mindy said.

"They're moving out of the office!" Owen reported. "I can hear the door opening and closing behind them."

It was time for us to take action.

"Okay, are you guys ready?" I asked.

Everyone nodded.

We left the Geek Cave and stood in the doorway just outside the cafeteria. Down the hall I could see the Pep Liaison coming our way. I could also see all the other students' tests in his bag. Next to him were Nerf, Weasel, and Mud. We needed to get to them, but first we needed to get to Darth Susan.

Unless our tests were included with the others, we were doomed.

Darth Susan always takes the south hall to get to the

security hole. So LAME darted across the hall and ran through the empty auditorium. We all made it to the doorway of the AntiSocial Studies hall and hid ourselves behind Tyler's supply and trash castle. If our calculations were correct, and most of our calculations are, Darth Susan would be coming in our direction any moment. We quickly worked on a plan.

What we were going to do wasn't too complicated. As soon as Darth Susan got close, I would shut off the hall lights. Then Mindy would aim, clap, and break Darth Susan's glasses. Being in the dark without glasses, she wouldn't be able to see anything. The second her glasses fell to the ground, I would jump out and grab the tests from her bag. Then before she knew what had happened, we would be out of the school and tracking down the Pep Liaison.

Darth Susan was getting closer. She was holding Becky over her shoulder.

We all held our breath. Mindy began softly counting down to herself.

"Five, four, three, two, one."

It was time.

Mindy reached her hands out from around the trash cans and clapped. At that same moment, I imagined the lights being off.

The hall went dark, and Darth Susan hollered.

"My glasses!"

Mindy's power had worked. Owen stepped out right in front of her and flashed his eyes.

The blinding light startled her, and she dropped Becky and fell to her knees. Owen kept flashing his eyes to make things even more confusing.

Darth Susan was screaming for Becky. She grasped at the floor and air, trying to find her lizard.

Unfortunately, instead of grabbing Becky, she grabbed Xen.

She picked Xen up and flung him over her shoulder. I thought she was going to spank him, but with her glasses off, she thought he was Becky.

I saw our four tests sticking out of her bag and grabbed them as Xen cried in her arms. I unzipped the front of my costume and put the tests inside. I zipped it back up. Owen and Mindy picked Becky up off the floor, and as gently as they could, they tossed her directly at Darth Susan.

The lizard collided into Darth Susan and Xen, and all three of them fell to the floor. Xen squirmed away while Becky scratched at both of them.

"Ahhh!" Xen cried.

"Becky? You can speak!" Darth Susan said excitedly.

Mindy helped Xen up, and the four of us took off down the hall, leaving a disoriented and blind Darth Susan to wrestle with her lizard alone in the dark hall.

We all squeezed through the security hole.

"That was way too close!" Mindy yelled.

"You're telling me!" Xen replied.

"Where's the liaison?" I asked Owen.

"I can hear him driving, and from the sound of things, they're more than halfway to the District Compound."

I should have done it earlier, but quickly I thought of turning off his car.

"What do you hear now?" I asked.

"A lot of swearing," Owen reported. "He's starting his car back up."

I turned it off again.

I ended up turning it off with my mind five times before Owen said that Peppy had given up and gotten out of the vehicle. He could hear him telling Nerf and the others that they were going to have to walk the rest of the way to the District Compound.

We had no time to waste.

Being heroes is not always easy. And sometimes it's disgusting.

CHAPTER SIXTEEN

Striking a Blow

It was overcast and already growing dark as the sun was covered with polluted clouds. The air was charged with a tinge of static electricity.

I saw a couple of cars driving on the street and imagined them turned off. They all shut down and rolled to a stop, making it a little easier for us to dash up the road.

"Can you still hear the Pep Liaison?" Xen yelled to Owen while trying to manage the group.

"Yes," Owen said. "They're down Bleak Street and just over that hill."

"We need to move faster," Mindy ordered. "The District Compound's at the end of Bleak Street. If they turn those tests in without ours, we're done for."

As much as we wanted to move faster, we were all hurting. It had been a long time since I'd run this much, and I was pretty sure that I was in better shape than the rest of LAME. Still we tried to move as quickly as we could even while Owen hacked up stuff, Mindy wheezed, and Xen whimpered.

"What are we going to do when we reach them?" Mindy asked.

"If we reach them," Xen said, huffing.

"We just have to distract them long enough to slip our four tests into Pep Liaison's bag. I'm hoping when they see us in our costumes, they'll tremble. Then, while they're trembling, we can put them in."

"So most likely we're doomed," Mindy said with worry.

"Keep going!" was my only reply.

Moving down Bleak Street wasn't easy, and when the road turned uphill, it was impossible to keep up a good pace.

"We're never going to catch them," Xen yelled.

"Is that the kind of attitude that Peppy would like?" Mindy yelled back.

"It's just that mathematically, at the pace we're going, we will never reach them before they reach the District Compound," Xen said, defeated. "I mean if x equals the speed we're running, and y equals the space between us and them. And if a equals the distance—"

"Stop talking and keep running!" I pleaded.

Just before reaching the top of the hill Owen took a break from hacking and wheezing to try to speak.

"There . . . is . . . something . . . happening," he wheezed. "Something's wrong . . . up ahead."

"What?" Mindy asked.

"I . . . can . . . still . . . hear Peppy and Nerf, but . . . now . . . they're screaming and fighting!"

"With each other?" Xen yelled.

"No, something else."

We reached the top of the hill, and I could see what Owen was talking about. On the road below us, the Pep Liaison, Nerf, Mud, and Weasel were all being attacked by a large crowd of Fanatics.

LAME stopped in our tracks and stared down the hill.

It was unusual for Fanatics to have formed groups and be roaming the streets so early. But the sky was getting darker, and Mr. Pep's group was currently getting the snot scratched and flashed out of them. The massive gaggle of

Fanatics had obviously ambushed them. We stood on the top of the hill, confused and worried. To make matters worse, Marsha was in the group—the leader of Marsha Law. She was currently taking pictures and harassing the Pep Liaison. Just seeing her made all hope disappear.

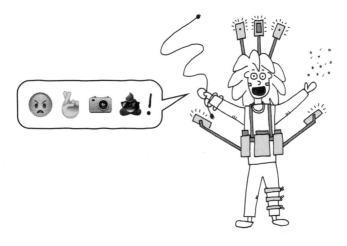

"What do we do?" Owen asked Xen.

"Don't look at me. I have no idea how to manage stuff like this. My recommendation is for us to run away."

"Maybe we should," Mindy said. "If we get involved, Marsha will pick us apart."

I looked at my three friends as we all stood nervously.

We really fit our name. All our costumes were kind of

lame, and our superpowers didn't really make us super. In fact, on a good day an above-average person might have been able to hear, clap, and think as well as us.

We were clearly out of our league.

Life had picked on us and teased us and ignored us for so long that it seemed like running and hiding might be the best solution (as usual). The world was a scary and confusing place. Why make it more complicated? People had messed with Marsha and felt the wrath.

The Fanatics began to really go at Peppy and Nerf.

"Should we cry for help, or just cry?" Owen asked.

I was seconds away from turning around and running away when I remembered the last line Dindo the elf king had said in the end of the first *Elf Scrimmage* book.

May your courage be as strong as the bad breath of Odderon!

"We should help," I blurted out.

"What!" Xen cried. "There's too many of them, and MARSHA."

"I know, but we can't just leave. We're LAME. We have to help them and then get our tests to the District Compound. We aren't the four puny geeks we were last week. Now we're geeks with attitude and weird powers. Mindy, you clap. Owen, you barrel into people and flash your eyes, and Xen, you manage the turd out of this thing."

"But we're afraid," Owen said.

I looked at all three of them. There was only one thing left for me to say.

May your courage be as strong as the bad breath of Odderon!

They smiled weakly and I smiled back. I turned and yelled "charge!" in Dindo's native elf tongue:

"Plinky!"

We barreled down the hill as fast as we could, letting momentum help us run faster than we would normally be able to. The Fanatics were tearing into Nerf and his friends with phone flashes and slap-chats, and the Pep Liaison was being pummeled but still trying to make things seem positive.

When we were inches away, we all screamed like we were on fire.

Everyone glanced in our direction.

I could be wrong, but it looked like some of the Fanatics

were intimidated. It was now our job to make sure they couldn't see how scared we really were.

I saw that Nerf was pinned and being forced to smile for selfie after selfie while Mud and Weasel were getting bludgeoned, which is an above-average way of saying smacked around with flashes and fists.

Mindy clapped into action!

A loud *crack* sounded. Every selfie stick that anyone was holding shattered and fell to the ground. Owen tripped and rolled into a girl who was trying to hit me with the third book in the Sand Thrower series.

She fell over and sprang right back up. Owen flashed his bright eyes, blinding her while Mindy and I took on a girl taking rapid-fire pictures, a boy using a tablet as a shield, and another girl whipping people with her charge cord.

I thought of every phone in the gathering and imagined them turning off. Instantly, dozens of Fanatics stopped what they were doing to stare helplessly at their dead phones. There was wailing and gnashing of teeth as everyone tried to figure out what was happening.

Nerf crawled up off the ground and scrambled behind us for protection. I don't think he knew who we were. Mud and Weasel moved back behind us too—Peppy did the same. The Fanatics were staring at their blank phones, looking shocked.

For a moment, I thought we had done it. We had swooped in and shut them all off. But as the Fanatics began to realize that their phones were dead, they looked at us with hatred in their eyes.

Spitting mad, they advanced toward us. Marsha moved to the front and stared me down.

There were just too many of them. There was nothing left for me and Mindy to break or turn off. Owen opened his eyes wide, but seeing someone with glowing eyeballs didn't slow them at all.

The Fanatics made a circle around us and began to close in tighter and tighter.

Mindy clapped at one wearing glasses, and the window of a car parked down the street shattered. I quickly started the car with my mind, but I couldn't drive it. I stopped a moving car that was driving around us, but that did us no good. The person driving just got out and ran away.

I wanted to run away too, but we were surrounded.

"Don't worry," I hollered. "They can't get us all."

"Really?" Mindy hollered back. "I think they can."

Xen began to burp. I didn't blame him. I was more frightened than I had been with the spiders crawling all over me. Was this how my life was going to end? Me, wearing a dumb homemade costume, hanging out with Nerf, and surrounded by angry Fanatics?

Marsha moved forward. She raised her book and screamed emojis at me.

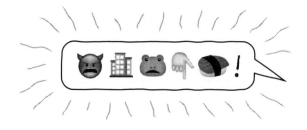

Xen burped again, and this time it was louder.

As he belched, the force of it knocked him backward and off his feet. Owen and I bent down to help him up, and when he stood, I saw that Marsha and four of the Fanatics who had been standing in front of Xen were now lying on the ground.

"What's—"

Before I could get my question out, Xen burped again, and the sound was deep and thumped the air like a giant drum. He flew back into me and Owen, while the Fanatics standing nearby were blown off their feet.

"Holy belching!" Owen screamed.

"Grab Xen's other arm!" I screamed back.

The two of us held on to Xen's arms and directed his head and body toward the frantic Fanatics now coming from behind us. Xen burped and it was so powerful we could barely keep him standing.

Waves of Fanatics toppled like dominoes.

"Everyone stay behind Xen!" I yelled. "He's blowing them all down!"

Mindy, Peppy, Nerf, Mud, and Weasel all scrunched in behind Xen, propping him up with all of our body weight.

The burping was coming at an abrupt and sudden pace now. We all held on to Xen and turned him in a circle. As he swiveled, Fanatic after Fanatic was blown down and over. They fell to the ground crying and wailing. One girl just kept yelling hashtags.

Hashtag life is unfair. Hashtag burps stink. Hashtag my nose is broken.

Some tried to stand and make another run at us, but each time, Xen was ready and blew them away. Marsha looked beat-up and out for blood.

Xen belched like he'd never belched before. It blew her back and onto her rear. It took a ton of smelly burps but eventually every last Fanatic had had enough and crawled off in defeat.

When all was said and belched, it was just me and Owen and Mindy and Xen standing while Nerf and Mud and Weasel and Peppy were crouched together behind us.

We turned to look at them, and Nerf stared up in amazement.

"Who are you?" he asked.

I couldn't believe it! He really didn't know who we were.

"We're—" Owen started to answer.

I slapped him on the back to shut him up before he ruined everything by telling the truth.

"We're the League of Average and Mediocre Entities," I said using a slightly altered voice. As I said it, I pointed to the logo on the front of my costume.

Nerf actually looked impressed.

We helped them all up, and as they were dusting themselves off, we tried to stand and pose in a position that we thought would look cool.

The Pep Liaison was impressed. He had smiled through the whole battle, but now he was grinning ear to ear.

"How can we ever thank you?" he asked. "Perhaps a hug?"

"That won't be necessary," I insisted.

Well then, we must run. I have some tests to drop off.

The tests!

I had forgotten what our mission was. Our tests needed to be put in his bag with the rest of them. But Mr. Peppy was beginning to walk away. I quickly unzipped my costume and pulled out the tests. Then, holding the papers behind me, I said . . .

"Wait! I'll take that hug after all."

The Pep Liaison turned and smiled. He then opened his

arms. I gave him a hug, and as I did, I slipped the four tests I had taken from Darth Susan into Peppy's bag with the others. The hug lasted a full five seconds before he let go.

"See?" he said to me. "Hugs make things better."

The tests were now tucked in his bag with the others. We just needed to get away before anyone realized what we had done or who we really were.

"We must go," I declared. "When the morrow comes, we will be nothing but wind."

"Is that a fart joke?" Owen whispered to me.

"No, I'm trying to be dramatic," I whispered back.

"It's working."

The four of us turned to leave but Nerf stopped us.

"Hold on a second," he said.

I stopped moving and slowly turned to look at him. I tried not to appear nervous as he studied my costume. He stared at me and cocked his head.

"I have a question."

I gulped as quietly as I could. Nerf was onto us, and this hard, messy, and terrifying day wasn't quite yet over.

"Yes?" I said with a deep voice.

Nerf gulped and said, "Um . . . do you think I could maybe join up with you guys?"

"What?" I asked, baffled.

"Your group," he said. "You guys are amazing. I don't have any powers, but I'm pretty good at fighting, and I'm willing to hit things. Just ask anyone."

"It's true," Weasel confirmed.

I was dumbfounded. Nerf still had no idea who we were. I put my hand on his shoulder and stared at him like my dad did when he was trying to be serious.

"Listen," I said. "This is not an easy life. The world is in turmoil. There are people who need help every second of the day. The government's corrupt, Fanatics rule the streets, the weather's a mess, and the only way you can get frosting is on the black market."

"I know all of that," Nerf said. "But I can help."

I looked at Nerf and wondered what he would do if he knew it was me. He'd most likely punch me and then steal my clothes and leave me in my underpants to walk home.

"So can I join?" he asked.

"No. Not right now."

Nerf looked crushed.

"But," I said, "maybe when the time is right, there will be a place for you in our group."

I took my hand off Nerf's shoulder and turned to run. The four of us then darted into the darkening afternoon and away from our first LAME victory. It had been a long few days, and the only mission we wanted to be a part of now was a mission to sleep.

CHAPTER SEVENTEEN

Secrets

"Tip?" Mr. Scrum asked. "Can you tell me why it's important to bury any money you might have?"

I thought a moment and then answered, "Because the banks are full of crooks, and most thieves don't like to take the time to dig things up."

Correct, Tip. Very good.

It had only been a day since the big test and the burp fight. I was sitting in my third-hour Conspiracy class and it was coming to an end. That meant lunchtime was near.

I had gotten to school early today because I wanted to find out our fate. I needed to see if our mission had worked and our school had passed the SLAP. If not, I knew we would all be attending outpost #72. But to my surprise, there had been no morning announcements and no mention of anything from any of the teachers or Finn about how well we had done.

Mindy was sitting at the desk to my right, and Owen and Xen were sitting a couple of rows up and over. My mind was racing a million miles an hour. (Sure, minds don't race—they send electronic impulses—but it felt like my brain was revving itself up.) I had no idea if Darth Susan had figured out that it was us who had taken back our tests and returned them to the Pep Liaison. And I didn't know if the District Compound had tallied, which is a goofy way of saying computed, the test scores yet.

I could see Mud sitting a couple of rows over, but there was no sign of Nerf. He usually sat to the left of me in Conspiracy class, but today his desk was empty.

Mr. Scrum asked Mindy if she knew the difference between the deceased and the undead. Mindy was about to answer but she was stopped by the sound of the school intercom crackling to life as Darth Susan spoke.

She sounded like a bummed-out Darth Vader. There was no pep in her pronunciation, and she was sniffling.

"I'm sorry to say this," she continued. "But due to circumstances beyond my control we . . . passed the SLAP."

Her words were followed by sobbing. I looked over at Mindy and smiled slowly. WE HAD DONE IT. Little did Darth Susan know that the very people she loved—Nerf and the Jocks—had helped Mr. Peppy turn in our tests and save the school.

"Also," Darth Susan went on, "today's lunch will be

squirrel jerky and canned mushrooms with almost a full piece of bread."

There was more crying, and then the intercom clicked off.

"We really did it," I mouthed silently to Mindy.

Mindy held her fingers up to her forehead to make the loser sign, but this time it stood for LAME. Or maybe it was for love? No, it was LAME.

I looked over at Owen and Xen and gave them the LAME sign too.

At that moment, the door to our classroom opened and Nerf stepped in. He handed his blue late slip to Mr. Scrum and stood there while our teacher studied it. Nerf didn't seem quite the same. He looked less obnoxious than usual. Also he was wearing something strange.

What?! Nerf had on a LAME T-shirt that looked like he had made himself. All our jaws dropped.

Nerf came down the row and sat in his desk next to mine.

I usually tried as hard as I could not to talk to him, but as soon as I had the chance, I leaned over and whispered, "What's on your T-shirt?"

He turned and stared at me.

"Really?" he said with a scoff. "It's only the coolest group of heroes ever. I can't believe you don't know what LAME is."

Nerf turned back around and listened to Mr. Scrum talk about how the government was sending radio waves into our heads to make us more obedient.

The subject interested me, but I was too busy thinking about Nerf's shirt to focus. Nerf had no idea that the very people he idolized were the same ones he was always picking on. I really wanted to tell him the truth, but the secret of LAME had to be kept.

Mr. Scrum instructed us to take out some tinfoil and make a hat so that the government couldn't steal our brainwaves. As I was making my hat, I overheard Mud talking to Nerf.

"Hey, Nerf," Mud said, "I heard that a bunch of Sox will be having a sock-sliding party in Q Hall during lunch. What say you, me, and Weasel bust it up?" Mud pounded his fist into his palm for emphasis.

"I don't know," Nerf replied. "Things are different. I mean, what about yesterday?"

"Yesterday was yesterday," Mud said. "Do we have to be lame now because of that? Maybe you didn't hear me—the Sox are having a sliding party. Plus, Tyler just waxed the floors. Those Sox will really travel when we push them around."

Nerf shrugged. "All right."

"So you're in?" Mud asked.

"I'm in," Nerf said with a smile.

I glanced at Mindy and then at Owen and Xen. Sure, we were Geeks, and yes, we had not been invited to the Sox sliding party, but everyone deserved justice, and now we're just the people to administer it.

Finn the crier cried out.

It's lunchtime! Also the wolf found in the girls' bathroom has been relocated. **All is well!**

I smiled. Not because Otto Waddle Jr. High Government Outpost was safe for the moment, and not because I had just finished making a really cool tinfoil hat. No, the reason for my smile was that, for the first time in our lives, me and my friends had a party to crash.

We just needed to make one quick change.

COMING SOON

Book 2 in the

series!

Being heroes is not always easy. And sometimes it's disgusting.

Mindy helped Xen up, and the four of us took off down the hall, leaving a disoriented and blind Darth Susan to wrestle with her lizard alone in the dark hall.

We all squeezed through the security hole.

"That was way too close!" Mindy yelled.

"You're telling me!" Xen replied.

"Where's the liaison?" I asked Owen.

"I can hear him driving, and from the sound of things, they're more than halfway to the District Compound."

I should have done it earlier, but quickly I thought of turning off his car.

"What do you hear now?" I asked.

"A lot of swearing," Owen reported. "He's starting his car back up."

I turned it off again.

I ended up turning it off with my mind five times before Owen said that Peppy had given up and gotten out of the vehicle. He could hear him telling Nerf and the others that they were going to have to walk the rest of the way to the District Compound.

We had no time to waste.